Raising the Subject

Robert Wystagon

The characters and events portrayed in this book are fictitious. Any similarity to real persons, living or dead, is coincidental and not intended by the author.

ISBN-978-1-0369-1234-5

Summer

'Are you happy here, Roy?'

Happiness. The word often featured in those reading books he'd rescued from the skip. It's what everyone was searching for. Was love the answer? Or was it fatal to true happiness? He knew it was something you had to seize. He'd have to check the quotations.

'I said, are you happy here?'

'Yes, Mrs King.'

'I want you to know that you're well-liked by everyone in the hospice. All the nursing staff. The patients. Agnieszka said she wouldn't be able to manage without you. So, this marks the end of your probationary period.'

'That's good, isn't it?'

'It certainly is.'

The hospice manager pushed two copies of the employment contract across her desk. Roy dragged his chair closer and ran his finger along the printed lines.

‘Agnieszka will go through the contract with you.’ She pointed at two yellow arrow stickers. ‘Just sign here and here.’

Roy settled the pen in his left hand and carefully formed each letter.

***

CHAPTER ONE

The Beeches was not easy to find. A faded sign on the pillared entrance was the only clue to its existence. Many people overshot on their first visit and ended up on the neighbouring caravan site. The original trees were long gone. They'd been replaced with a row of evergreens, to shield the hospice from public view all year round. Those who ventured between the pillars on foot could read the dozens of commemorative plaques set into the path – a processional roll call for those who spent their last days here. A rose-covered pergola shrouded the entrance, where silent automatic doors ushered visitors inside. The ground floor was particularly confusing for visitors, with its ill-fitting building extensions and illogical, dead-end corridors. Paint was beginning to peel off the cream-coloured walls. The worn lino flooring was held together with duct tape. Corroded window frames kept the air stale.

Roy was completely at ease within the building. What had seemed so alien to him on that freezing February day when he first arrived, was now his turf: his second home. Every corridor, step, slope and turning was mapped; no-one knew the layout better than him. Bounding down three flights of service stairs, Roy sang a jingle he'd heard on local radio that morning. He vaulted over the last handrail and entered the ground floor. Checking his jacket pocket for the folded contract, he considered his good fortune. It had all seemed like luck to him – a room above the florist, the delivery of some wreathes, then a full-time job. 'They're gold dust,' his line manager Agnieszka often reminded him, her hands placed together in prayer. Pausing at the laundry door, Roy watched two Filipino women, quietly singing a traditional love song, as they folded bedsheets together. They smiled at each other, without acknowledging their young admirer. A sharp left turning and a skip down three shallow steps brought Roy to his domain. The facilities room was half office and half workshop, every surface piled high with items in need of repair. This week, plastic crates were filling with bed wheels and motors. It was curious how they all failed at the same time. Roy removed a G-clamp from a recently glued garden chair and spun it around to his cluttered desk. He checked his mobile for missed calls, then started to read aloud the Confirmatory Medical Certificate in his tray.

'Mrs Emily Spears. When did you last see deceased alive? 03:45. Mode of death, exhaustion.' He struggled with the cause of death, sounding each syllable. 'Met-a-stat-ic-ad-en-o-car-cin-o-ma, of unknown primary.'

The reek of tobacco preceded Agnieszka through the open door. The facilities manager lit another tea light from a spluttering wick and watched the flame settle.

'Angie? You all right?'

'Emily Spears. Side Room Five.'

'With the young daughter,' Roy recalled. 'Nice woman. She always waved when I went by.'

'I've put her things into a crate, just inside the door. Will you?'

'Will do.'

'Have you done the salt?'

'Check.'

'Fire alarm test at twelve.'

It happened every week, but Roy's heart always sank a little: thirty-six automatically closing doors to reset.

'I've got my contract of employment. Mrs King said you'd go through it with me.'

Agnieszka unfolded the document and winced at the column of formal paragraphs.

'Oh, Roy, I only just understood my own. I would, you know, but ...'

'That's fine,' answered Roy brightly, returning the pages to his pocket.

Side Room Five was one of eight first-floor rooms on the outside of the building. Being moved to a room with a view indicated that your time was short. Passing the doors, Roy glanced at the motionless occupants. He grabbed the crate from Side Five and cut through one of the central wards, where dormitory-like beds were mostly occupied. One thin arm was raised and a voice croaked.

'Roy. Legend.'

'All right?'

'Tip top, but the light woke me before dawn.'

Roy switched the flickering night light on and off.

'Needs a new starter. I'll see to that.'
The William Tell Overture blared from Roy's mobile.

Agnieszka disliked the mortuary. For someone uncomfortable with the dead and dying, working in a hospice seemed like a strange vocation. On Roy's first day in February, she had fumbled with her long chain, attempting to select the right key. Roy had noticed that her hand was shaking.

'So cold now, isn't it?'

What Roy experienced first was the smell. It was sweet and not unpleasant: detergent and disinfectant, with a hint of decay. The green-tinted fluorescent tube hummed quietly, supplemented by the colder winter light seeping through an air grille, set high on the whitewashed wall.

'I expect you want to see inside.'

Agnieszka had hesitated, before pulling on a huge lever, like a one-armed bandit, and opening the heavy refrigerator door. Two bodies were visible inside, their mottled bare feet sticking out of the gloom. A third body, on the top shelf, was sealed in a translucent plastic sleeve.

'Why's that one in a bag?' Roy had asked.

'It's a precaution. You know, sometimes they have an infection. The nurses will explain that to you.' Agnieszka muttered something in Polish, as she closed the door firmly. Roy gestured to a pale green door on the opposite wall.

'And what's through there?'

'Another time.'

Today, like most days, it was Roy who met the undertakers, who were already standing either side of the mortuary door. The long-faced pair could have been twin brothers, able to stand motionless like bookends. Reddington Funeral Directors had enjoyed a long and successful partnership with the hospice. Their reliability and affordable funeral plans had always been an easy sell to visiting patients and relatives. An undertaker twisted his head in an exaggerated manner to read the book titles under Roy's arm.

'*Welcome Temptation*. Romance ... that's a new genre for you, Roy.'

'Emily Spears.'

'Ah, the very person we've come for.'

The undertakers took each end of their trolley and followed Roy into the mortuary. He checked the paperwork.

'Left. Middle shelf.'

With familiar ease, they pulled on latex gloves and extracted the body, sliding it effortlessly on steel rollers. Within seconds, Emily was inside a temporary coffin. The undertakers disposed of their gloves and handed Roy a few pound coins. They steered the trolley through the service door and into their grey private ambulance.

'Fire alarm is just a test,' bellowed Roy, over the loud siren; none of the semi-conscious patients cared one way or another. He passed the first-floor nurses' station as the alarm stopped. Precious Adaugo uncovered her ears.

'Dear Lord. Why does it have to go on for so long?'

'I don't know. I'll find out for you, if you want.'

'I do want. And bring me your answer,' smiled the Nigerian nurse with mock seriousness. Resetting the doors usually created more maintenance jobs. Today, it was a detached hinge and a scattering of broken screws. The smell of cooking wafted up the service stairway.

'Roast on Monday, curry on Wednesday and fish on Friday,' chanted Roy.

Returning to the workshop, he dropped the pound coins into a glass jar. This small ritual exchange for the body either brought good luck or deflected bad luck; Roy couldn't remember which. Either way, the jar was always half full or half empty. Agnieszka said she used the money to buy small gifts for the patients.

The sharp scent of vinegar filled the corridor. Roy ran his finger along gouges in the wall, made by various trolleys. Lunch over, the cook was taking five, while her staff clattered and chattered in the kitchen. Bernice insisted that her eighty kilos were all muscle. She'd done a bit of tag wrestling at the local holiday camp and had a few frayed flyers to prove it. She also still had the two-tone crewcut that had intimidated her opponents.

'Sit down, Roy. You're always running around like a blue-arsed fly.'

Roy joined Bernice for their daily ritual. He removed the aluminium plate cover, leaned backwards and swallowed a chip whole.

'Nice,' purred Roy.

'You learn that from the seagulls?'

He opened his new contract of employment. Bernice scanned the pages as he ate.

'Six months. That's gone quickly.'

'Is it all right?'

'Holiday. Pension contribution. Confidentiality. Giving notice. Bog standard. Did you ask for a raise?' Roy stopped chewing, genuinely concerned. 'Only kidding, you're all right. The supermarket called. They've got half a pallet for us.'

'I'll collect it after the home run.'

'Tomorrow's fine. Oh no, it's Saturday.'

'Today's fine.'

'If they give you bread, leave all of the white sliced. It only ends up in the bin. It attracts the foxes.'

Three-twenty was going home time. At three o'clock, every week day, Roy parked the minibus at the main entrance. He followed the checklist taped to the inside of the rear door, ensuring the sidestep, seatbelts, wheelchair straps and tail lift were all sound and secure. Opening his transport sheet, Roy ran through the Friday route in his mind. There would be mumbled complaints about the roads taken and the order of dropping off, but he knew he was helping all of his passengers on their journey – Mrs King had told him so. The day centre was on the second floor. The descent was a lengthy affair, with a wheelchair, sticks, walking frames and a wilful lift. The caravan meandered slowly towards the entrance in silence. As the day patients bagged their favourite seats, Roy rode the minibus tail lift with a sour-looking man.

'I know you.' An accusatory finger wagged before Roy's face. 'Always hanging around this place.'

'Roy.'

'Roy, that's right. Remembered your name, have you?'

'What's he on about?' asked a new passenger. One of the regulars made the loco gesture near her temple.

'Alzheimer's.'

The chairbound ex-policeman pointed at his fellow passengers.

'I'll be taking statements.'

Roy secured the chair, checked everyone's seat belt, then slid into the driving seat. A chubby woman straightened her wig and pulled on an imaginary train whistle cord.

'Toot toot. The stage four coach is leaving.'

'No-one thinks that's funny,' the new passenger commented.

'Control your passengers, driver,' added Frances from the back row.

Roy checked his favourite passenger in the rear-view mirror and smiled. The sixty-year-old blonde was wearing a black cape, her face half hidden by the hood. She swigged from her hip flask and winked at Roy.

'And keep your eyes on the road.'

The seaside resort had been growing for two hundred years. Behind the Georgian seafront properties and the Victorian town, post-war developers had added a wide skirt of cul-de-sacs; thousands of identical bungalows lying low: keen to be inconspicuous. Poets, artists, flowers and trees had all given their names to the suburban developments. The detective was set down on Wordsworth Close,

The thin, tearful girl on Stubbs Lane and Frances in Rose Gardens. Roy wended his way to surrounding farmhouses, then sped to the retail park. He backed into the supermarket delivery bay.

'Is Larry here?'

A weary worker pinched off a half-finished cigarette, gave her cashier smile and shouted under the shutter.

'Larry. Hospice man for you.'

Larry had loaded the groceries carelessly. By the time Roy got back to the hospice, burst yoghurt pots had spilled their contents across the minibus floor. On the far side of the carpark, Roy hosed down the vehicle's interior and sang along with local radio hits. The sound of knocking drew his attention to a first-floor window, where a nurse was waving. He remembered that he'd promised to fix the ward's night light before going home. He acknowledged, then looked at a side room window. Despite the bright afternoon sun reflecting off the glass, he was just able to discern a slim face, returning his gaze. The features retreated into the room and disappeared from view. On the first floor, Roy tried the door of Side Room

Six, where a curtain was drawn across the observation panel. He located the master key on his chain and entered. Side Six had not been used for months. Agnieszka had insisted that the cracked flooring needed replacing, then said the shower was unsafe to use. Roy knew they were excuses – she was frightened of the room; she thought it was haunted. The air was still and dust hovered in the golden afternoon glow. He checked the adjoining bathroom, then crossed to the window and looked down to the carpark. He must have been mistaken. It must have been a trick of the light. Roy double-checked the room was locked, before leaving.

CHAPTER TWO

Gina's was perfectly situated, opposite the town cemetery and crematorium. Flowers for all occasions, read the banner above the shopfront, but wreathes and memorial vases were Gina's bread and butter. To one side of the handsome window display, a narrow side door opened onto a vertiginous staircase. With his bike over one shoulder, Roy made easy work of the steps, up to his room. Originally a storeroom over the shop premises, the bedsit had restricted headroom on one side and a whole wall of shelving. It was the empty shelves that had sold the place to Roy. Back in the children's home, owning a book marked you out for punishment. Here, Roy was able to build his library in safety. Fiction went on the lowest shelf, in order of difficulty. Higher up, books were stacked according to his own categories, each neatly labelled: history, nature, people, places to go and things to do. The middle shelves were filled with Roy's favourite journal: one-hundred issues of Reader's Digest, donated by a patient. Each cover promised gripping, human-interest stories and they'd never let him down; good people had such courage, battling, fighting and overcoming adversity. Quotations and sayings were of particular interest. Roy had cut them out and ordered them separately in a shoebox: success is falling nine times and getting up ten; champions keep playing until they get it right; a real friend is one who walks in when the rest of the world walks out.

Roy's bedsit was always shipshape. He was delighted with his foldaway galley kitchen. He stowed his groceries, kicked off his boots and sat at the helm, in the window bay. He basked in the warm evening air and listened to Gina, chatting to a late customer in the shop below. He'd heard her sales pitch many times before. To help people choose a tribute, she would explain the significance of each bloom. Red roses spoke of passionate love, while pink roses suited friendship – yellow for zeal and white for purity. Daisies for innocence and the peony for healing. Whether it was the warmth on his face or Gina's soothing voice, Roy relaxed for the first time that day.

‘Roy?’

Roy was curled awkwardly on his narrow bed, still dressed. He blinked against the morning light and opened his window. Gina stood in the yard below, scrolling through the orders on her iPad.

‘Good morning, my love. Three services today. First one is eleven-twenty.’

With her collection of garish floral blouses and overpowering perfumes, it was as if Gina was trying to compete with her flowers. She had outlived two husbands, so she knew the crematorium well, but it was Roy who went there on Saturdays. He loaded the small delivery van and drove slowly through the cemetery. Behind the squat, redbrick building, he placed the flowers on a long shelf, reading the names of the deceased to put them in order. Each ceremony was allocated forty minutes. The crematorium staff steered straggling mourners behind a wall of rhododendrons and ushered people in for the next service. The flower arrangements were similarly swapped. Tributes that had taken florists hours to prepare returned to the bay for composting. Roy was sometimes tempted to load them back into the van; each one could make a few bouquets. He watched the new set of mourners, awkward in their hired suits and borrowed dresses. There would always be one person who laughed too often and too loud, attempting to cheer-up the others and hide their own discomfort. Roy lingered, to watch the tearful embraces.

*

On the seafront, families littered the stony beach, whilst teenagers sought more racy pleasures in the amusement park. Roy leaned against his bike and watched screaming girls being catapulted high into the blue sky – XLR8, blinked the pulsating rainbow lights. He cycled along the pier and raised his hand to a couple of anglers, who whiled away their lives, sharing bait tips and sporting half-truths. At the edge of town, the promenade became scruffier. A large public shelter had been requisitioned by a homeless group. Two ancients were fighting over a sleeping bag. One drinker was shouting at an invisible adversary, lager spilling from his can. A youth on an undersized BMX appeared from behind the shelter and shot towards Roy, like a trapdoor spider after its prey.

'Wait up.'

The youth drew level. He threw his hoodie back, to reveal his bleached mullet and a crazed smile.

'Hello, friend ... what's your name?'

Before Roy could answer, the youth spotted a couple of policemen ahead and turned abruptly.

'Drop in. We're all friends,' his sing-song voice trailed. 'There's a party, and you're all invited.'

The coastal cycle path continued for another three miles. Roy once covered it in nine minutes, but today he had to steer clear of wandering children and wayward mobility scooters. His destination was the Seashell Café. The owner's wife had visited the hospice many times and Roy's money was no good here. Sitting at the best table, he listened to the chatter and laughter of holidaymakers. He drained his second cappuccino and copied text from the blackboard into his notebook – 'Homemade lunches and desserts'. He was keeping a diary for his weekly literacy class. His tutor had told him to leave nothing out. Roy wrote – one carrot cake and two coffees – adding the coloured chalk curlicues. He'd made a good start in the skills class. The other learners were friendly; perhaps he would find a friend there. In the late afternoon, beach life started a new chapter; sunburned children were herded up and some revellers arrived for an evening barbecue. Roy waited until dusk, then cycled along the seafront, undulating ribbons of decorative lanterns leading him back to town.

Opening the window in his room, Roy heard Gina talking to a visitor. Her voice was unusually bright and playful. She laughed like a girl. 'I entertain gentlemen,' she had once told Roy, 'You'll have to excuse the noise'. What had sounded so enjoyable at midnight, turned in to a heated row. Roy was relieved when doors were slammed in the small hours and Gina listened to a talk radio station. He could hear that tonight's subject was friendship. He tuned in to the same programme.

Sunday did not live up to its name. Gulls perched on the groynes under a grey sky and the hardiest holidaymakers huddled behind flapping windbreaks. Roy cycled through the Municipal Gardens and locked his bike at the fortune teller's kiosk. Lace shrouded the little windows, but the palmist was not at home. He read the handwritten notice aloud.

'Closed due to illness.'

He was disappointed. Madame Kezia had been a friend for years. When he was a kid, Roy would do anything to be away from the children's home. He skipped school most days and usually ended up at this sanctuary. Madame always assured him good fortune and told him wild tales about her distant family. Roy did one circuit of the pier, greeted the anglers and meandered along the prom, away from the town centre. At the public shelter, he found evidence of its recent occupation. He stacked discarded cardboard bedding on the seat and tossed a few empty beer cans into the bin. The place smelled of piss. The glass wind protectors were covered in graffiti – scrawled messages of love and hate: either way someone was going to get it.

*

Sister Nielsen started her ward round at seven on the dot. Patients, who had spent the small hours trying to sleep, were roused by her shrill voice. It had been a busy night. Two deaths on the ground floor and one on the first required the quiet drawing of curtains and the discreet removal of bodies. Patients looked impassively at the empty beds – a daily reminder of their own position in the dreary queue. The priority now was pain management. Relief came from one flower, but in many forms: tablets, capsules, granules, suppositories and injections for all, each according to their need. After the opiates, dozens of parenteral treatments. Dressings were gingerly removed from weeping wounds and ulcers; colostomy bags were changed and ointments applied. For severe constipation, Precious Adaugo was the natural choice. She was the top bottom nurse, able to shift any obstinate stool.

When the front doors were unlocked at eight, fresh air snaked through the musty hospice corridors. The overnight rain had lowered the temperature and washed litter into one corner of the carpark. Although Roy had been instructed not to ride his bike inside the building, he could not resist seeing how far he could get each day – there was usually no-one about. This morning, Agnieszka was so absorbed in her phone rant, that she barely noticed the squealing brakes. She ended the call and shook her head.

'Men, they're all bastards. Not you, Roy.' Her cheek was swollen, the bloodshot eye a bruised orbit.

'You're hurt. What happened?' asked Roy.

'I walked into a door.'

'Really?'

'No, not really,' Agnieszka replied flatly. 'It's a saying, in everyone's language.'

'I didn't know that. Is there anything I can do?'

Agnieszka sighed and smiled. 'I need a cigarette.'

Steering his bike into the ground floor storeroom, Roy was startled by a loud banging on the metal exterior door. Unlocking it, he faced a surly delivery driver, who'd already stacked dozens of oxygen cylinders by the storage cage.

'I'll get the key.'

'Next time,' insisted the driver.

Roy checked the invoice. He recognised many of the words, but the listed sizes and quantities swam before his eyes. The driver tossed a pen onto the tailgate.

'Sign anywhere.'

It was the same every Monday. Most of the staff were in a bad mood and many things were not in their usual places. A drug dispensing trolley was leaning against the corridor wall, one wheel missing. Yellow sharps boxes and waste sacks were stacked by the workshop door. Roy reordered the keys in their metal wall safe, then stowed the delivery of gas cylinders. He heaved sacks of salt into the water softener and cleared the litter. At nine-fifteen, he collected his weekly schedule from Mrs King. Today, the usual passengers would be joined by a new day patient. The address was way out of town. He'd need to make an early start.

*

Lapwing Cottage nestled on the last bend of a creek, steep steps and a flint wall protecting it against the encroaching tide. A man stood at the front gate, looking out across the river. In his crumpled linen suit and felt hat, he looked as old as the stone building.

'Mr Devereux?'

The man tipped his hat to Roy and slowly descended the steps. Leaning heavily on his cane, he boarded the minibus and took the first available seat. Roy gestured to the back row.

'Do you mind sitting back here, Mr Devereux? Some of the patients are very choosy.'

A few seconds passed before Devereux moved to the offered seat.

'It's Devereux. Like the letter O.'

'Oh.'

As he drove along thc shore road, Roy's attempts to start a conversation were met with silence. The man lowered his head, as if to sleep. For the next fifty minutes, Roy meandered through twisting rows of silent bungalows, collecting his passengers: two wheelchairs, two delays ('Be out in a minute') was all too much for Devereux, who let out a long, loud moan. Faces turned to glimpse. Everyone seemed to hold their breath, as the ambulance lurched through the hospice entrance and came to an abrupt stop. Devereux was last off. He strode well behind his fellow passengers and lowered his hat for privacy in the lift. The day visitors took their favourite seats and waited to be served coffee by a handful of cheerful volunteers. An older patient with bouffant hair and pearls waited for a quiet word with the manager. She commented on the frightful journey and the borderline rudeness of the new gentleman. Roy steered the wheelchairs in to place and checked the level on a travelling oxygen cylinder. The large oval table and surrounding wingback chairs looked as if they'd been arranged for a séance.

CHAPTER THREE

With fundraising day approaching, memorial furniture needed to be lugged out of the cellar. Roy had to stoop in the dark, confined space. The acrid smell told him the feral cats were back. They regularly left the remains of their kills strewn across the bare soil, where brightly-coloured moulds and fungi sprouted. Garden benches were stacked tightly under a mildewed cover, every one bearing the name of a deceased patient. Roy used a torch to check the names on Agnieszka's list. It was important to select the right ones, as donors would be showing up and looking for their gift. It used to be an important day for The Beeches. Patients, staff and visitors could enjoy the outdoors and forget their own mortality for a few hours. A framed photograph in Mrs King's office showed her accepting a giant-size cheque from the local mayor. The hospice once had a magnificent garden, with winding pathways and arbours, but it was different now. Most of the land had been sold to property developers, whose starter homes now huddled behind a high fence. Only a small paved area remained. Roy blinked as he emerged into the light, a garden bench on one shoulder. Seated in the shade, Agnieszka used her dying cigarette to light a new one.

'These things will kill me. Don't you dare smoke.' She lifted her sunglasses, to smile at Roy, who was holding the garden bench with one hand. Her shiner shone under the noonday sun.

'Superman.'

Roy read from the list.

'Dearest Brenda. Heaven couldn't wait.'

'Pride of place. Her son's a big donor. Comes every year.' Roy carefully positioned the bench. 'Sit down. Relax.'

He perched uncomfortably on the edge of the bench, glancing at his phone, to check for messages.

'Angie? Do you think there is a heaven?'

'I hope so.'

'Does everyone go there? Do you think?'

Agnieszka rubbed her bruised eye. 'I hope not.'

'Is that what a ghost is? Someone who didn't get to heaven?'

'You've seen it.' she said softly, but with some urgency. Agnieszka confessed she'd never actually seen the ghost, but once she had heard about the haunting of Side Room Six, she too embellished the stories of unlocked doors, missing keys and strange whisperings. One nurse claimed that appearances were preceded by the smell of lavender – violets, insisted one of the cleaners. The apparition was short, tall, female, male, fast and slow moving. There were many candidates, of course. Since the hospice was opened in the mid-sixties, more than six hundred patients had died in Side Room Six.

'When was this?'

'Friday, when I was cleaning the bus.'

A barrage of questions followed: hair? height? complexion? clothing? Roy wanted to answer, but soon wished he'd never mentioned it.

'It's a sign. Someone's going to die.'

A dead cert, thought Roy.

Things were not going well in the day room. It had all started when the drinks trolley was wheeled in. After two large whiskies, Mr Devereux had levelled his cane like a hunting rifle and 'dispatched' a few of his fellow patients. Following a quiet word with Mrs King, he returned to the day room, doffed his hat in a conciliatory gesture and wandered off, in search of the lift. The remaining day visitors chattered excitedly. Some felt sure they recognised the man; he'd been on television, or in some magazine articles. Roy was summoned to drive Mr Devereaux home, but the man had already made his escape in a taxi. Roy ate his lunch alone, swabbed the mortuary floor, collected the post and delivered blood samples to the local surgery. At three-twenty, the Monday crowd boarded the minibus, sedated by alcohol and the blazing Sun. It was one of the quietest journeys Roy had ever taken. Not a soul could be seen in any of the silent cul-de-sacs. With one passenger left, he headed for Azalea Close. He recalled Gina's soothing sales pitch, that repeatedly echoed from the florist, 'Azaleas represent the care you take of yourself and those around you. The perfect flower for any funeral service'.

'She hates me.'

Roy glanced in the rearview mirror at the tearful woman, clinging tightly to her seatbelt.

'Is everything OK?'

'She hates my guts. Not that she'd tell me, to my face.'

'If there's anything ...'

'She switched off my freezer. Everything was ruined. Claimed it was an accident. Never mind, Marion, she said, you won't be needing it. Bitch.'

Roy had learned that it was best not to respond to anything said by patients, unless it was a direct question. With months or weeks to live, they would occasionally vent their suppressed frustrations, fears and regrets. It wasn't a question of candour; they were simply oblivious to the driver's presence.

As Roy cycled back through the Municipal Gardens, a figure from the past stepped onto the path, his arms outstretched. Roy remembered the bleached mullet and crazed smile.

'Friend.' Roy braked awkwardly. 'Nice bike. How many gears has it got?'

'Fourteen.'

'I don't think you're allowed to cycle in public gardens.'

'Everyone else does.'

'Someone could get hurt.'

'Beano ...'

The youth raised his hoodie and disappeared behind a privet. Roy pushed his bike forward to see the owner of the quiet, commanding voice. The thin man was thirty, but years of living rough had added a decade to his weathered face. Wearing a greatcoat and sprawled inside an arbour seat, he looked perfectly at home. Beano was huddled to one side, like a naughty child.

'We've seen you about,' observed the man, raising a weak smile. 'You look as if you might be useful.'

'I am useful,' replied Roy. He'd been told as much on many occasions.

'I think you could take care of yourself.'

The man gestured to a facing garden bench, as if it was in his office. Roy sat on the crossbar of his bike, uncertain.

'Napoleon. No relation. And this is my lieutenant, Beano.'

'Hello,' replied Roy.

'He's very polite, I bet you he ...'

Napoleon silenced Beano with a barely perceptible gesture.

'And your name is?'

'Roy.'

'And whereabouts do you live, Roy?'

'Up near the cemetery.'

'A nice quiet spot,' said Napoleon, without a smile. Beano swallowed his laughter. Napoleon continued. 'Do you have a phone?'

'For work. It's not mine.'

'Do you do Facebook?'

'No.'

'TikTok? and the rest?'

Roy shook his head, unsure of the question.

'Very wise,' interjected Beano. 'There are some right bastards out there.'

Napoleon raised a cautioning hand. Beano pulled his hood down. Rain pricked Roy's cheeks. He felt uncomfortable. Mrs King often advised him to be more cautious - 'discreet' she called it. The word was in his notebook - *showing discernment or good judgment in conduct and especially in speech: prudent.*

'I think I should be going,' suggested Roy.

'We'll see you around, then,' Napoleon replied softly.

Roy closed the front door of his bedsit with an elbow and carried his bike aloft. It wasn't just the heat slowing him down; he'd forgotten to eat his lunch. He unwrapped some huge slices of pizza and detached a greasy Post-it note from Bernice - *you need to eat more.* His appetite sated, he scraped the remaining granules from a jar of coffee and squirted the curdled contents of a milk carton down the sink. He thought about his disappointed passenger. Perhaps he should get a freezer: not a freezer but a fridge. He'd seen small ones at the hospice; he would ask Mrs King to check his savings. He settled in to his sunny seat at the window, drank weak, black coffee and listened to Gina as she sang enthusiastically: she must have sold a lot of flowers. This evening's Reader's Digest story was astounding. Despite having lost a leg and an arm in a motorcycle accident, Greg "mountain bear" Jackson had walked a 45-mile trail in Rocky Mountain National Park. Roy reached for his notebook and copied words from the hero's T-shirt: *non deficere.* Hours later, he woke to see two moths spinning noisily around his reading light.

*

Patients were dropping like flies. The hospice night staff wheeled three bodies to the mortuary in the small hours and pushed the release forms under the facilities room door: gliobastoma, metastatic adenocancinoma of the colon and astrollitoma. With three side rooms now vacant, Roy's first job of the day was to remove the patients' possessions and check that all lights and appliances were working normally. He returned with a mop and bucket. Sister Nielsen hovered in the doorway.

'Wrong bucket. Red is for washrooms. Has your manager not explained the colour code to you?'

'The yellow buckets are missing.'

'Find one. You've been here six months.'

'I'll clean it,' Roy assured her.

'If you want to make yourself useful, find a way of getting some air in here.'

Roy scraped paint and rust from the metal frames, then managed to prise a couple of windows open. Precious Adaugo steered her drugs trolley past the open door.

'Bless you, Roy.'

Agnieszka was secretly relieved by the overnight departures. It meant Side Room Six would not need to be re-commissioned this month; it would remain locked, blinds drawn. Roy realised he'd missed breakfast. He grabbed some leftover fried bread from the kitchen warming shelf and hit the trail. After his patient run, he drove to the Town Hall, where he waited for a new book of blank death certificates. He'd only recently been assigned to this task. Mrs King had explained that each and every certificate would be worth a fortune in the wrong hands; he 'must never let the book out of his sight'. As he waited in the registrar's reception, he watched a young couple enter and cross to the main desk. They reminded Roy of the mourners he observed regularly at the crematorium, with their unfamiliar formal clothes and bowed heads – perhaps they were here to register a death. After the checking of various documents, the couple sat directly opposite. Roy stared at the young, elfin woman, certain that he'd seen her somewhere before. The man returned Roy's stare and gave a V sign. The woman gently lowered her companion's hand and reached into her pocket for two ivory rose buttonholes: this was not a death registration, but a marriage.

Roy held the death certificate book tightly, as he ran up the hospice stairs. He presented it to Mrs King like a happy dog returning a stick to its owner. With lunchtime practically over, Roy had to rescue the last portion of curry. He found a table that didn't reek of disinfectant. Bernice joined him, carrying a stack of papadums.

'Here you go. No-one else seemed to like them.'

'Can I have two?'

'Three, four ... fill your boots.'

'You'll make me fat.'

'Fat chance. Look at you. I'm going to say it again ... wrestling.'

'You reckon?' replied Roy, with a broad smile.

'I can see you like the idea. Show us your biceps.' Roy struck a comic muscle-man pose. 'Honestly, you're wasted here. You could be king of the canvas. You'll need a good name,' added Bernice, as she pushed a bowl of trifle across the table.

Before he'd finished eating, Roy's vibrating mobile danced across the table. He was summoned to the mortuary to meet the undertakers from Reddington Funeral Directors, 'Right. Lower shelf'. As they turned to leave one of the undertakers leaned on the temporary coffin and folded his arms.

'Roy, how long have you been working here? Six months?'

'And five days.'

'Didn't I say so?' His colleague nodded solemnly. 'Time passes so quickly.'

Roy watched the facilities room wall clock, counting backwards as the second hand swept around. Agnieszka looked up from her keyboard and placed a silencing finger on her lips.

'Please ... I'm putting your numbers into my accounts. Shouldn't you be taking the patients home?'

'In one minute and thirty-seven seconds, thirty-six ...'

Only three patients had felt well enough for the Wednesday hospice day visit. Two women in their seventies sat together. A thin man slouched on the other side of the vehicle, looking closely at his discoloured hands.

'Driver? can we stop for a moment?' requested one of the women. 'There's a gap here, by the shelter.'

Roy parked the minibus and switched off the engine. 'Do you need a sick bowl?'

The woman shook her head and turned to the thin man. 'You don't mind, do you? Just for a minute or two?' The thin man gave a friendly smile and slid across to a sea-side seat. 'It's just that I used to play here. I lived just behind those houses.'

The woman pointed at an Edwardian terrace. All three passengers turned their gaze to the sunlit beach and remained silent, lost in thought. Returning to The Beeches, Roy parked directly towards the Sun, closed his eyes and enjoyed his own reverie. This was the moment he enjoyed most each day, able to muse quietly. He thought about the writing task he needed to complete before his next literacy class. Students had been asked to describe a happy day in the past using the five Ws guideline: *who, what, when, where* and *why*. 'A happy day?' he asked the empty minibus. 'Juliet. First sex. Sixteenth birthday. Care home. *Why?* why not. Three-hundred words. I can do that,' he announced.

Roy leant against his pillow, staring at four completed sentences and listened to the dawn chorus. He shoved the bedsheets into his backpack, carried his bike down the stairs and quietly locked the front door. He rode quickly through the deserted town, past shuttered arcades and sleeping fairground attractions. The morning air was refreshingly cool and invigorating; this was exactly what he needed to focus his thoughts. He sped through the shopping precinct, pausing only to bin some discarded fast food wrappers. Opening the hospice door required a few attempts. He'd never needed to use the overnight keycode. '2345,' he whispered repeatedly, as he cycled along the dim corridors. Roy emptied Agnieszka's ashtrays and raided her biscuit tin. Recalling his years spent in various care homes brought little joy. The daily menu was intimidation, deprivation and loneliness, and you had to suck it up. If it hadn't been for Juliet, he would probably have ended up on the street, like a couple of other residents. She was an old hand at the game – a troubled beauty, still young enough to keep signs of abuse on the inside. She'd made a beeline for Roy and had taken the minor under her wing.

'I'll fuck you on your sixteenth birthday. Don't want to get us in to any more trouble, do I?' She kept her promise: seven honeyed weeks of mutual desire. When the vindictive care home staff made a beeline for Juliet, she set fire to the curtains and ran away.

Roy was surprised how easily the words came in the end. He proudly placed the handwritten pages into his literacy class folder.

CHAPTER FOUR

Maria and Maria ruled the laundry room. Regularly humming Filipino melodies in the same key as the industrial washing machines and dryers, they folded the sheets and towels as if they were performing a national dance. Roy had always been slightly unnerved by the two women, who were the happiest and loudest in the building. Clutching his laundry, as if for protection, he entered their lair. The women laid his smalls out on the white sorting table as if they were tarot cards. Some coins were retrieved from a pair of trousers with a gentle admonishment.

'Bad luck ... throw fortune away,' said the Marias in unison.

The Thursday morning passengers were an unusually sanguine bunch, releasing their grievances as if they were paper lanterns. A bumpy detour along an unadopted road resulted in hoots of laughter and the gripping of safety rails; for a few moments, patients were able to enjoy their own fairground ride. Escorting the patients to the hospice day centre, Roy tried to avoid the Chaplain's attention. Making a hasty exit didn't work. The unctuous man fastened himself to Roy's arm and waited before speaking.

'Dear Roy, you're always in such a hurry. Please.'

The Chaplain steered Roy into the adjacent prayer room. The stale smell indicated how often the small, featureless room was used: six beige chairs faccd a commemorative book and two dusty plastic plants. The Chaplain gestured to a seat and sat facing.

'I do like this place. It's always so peaceful.'

'I have to go and collect the drugs ... the controlled drugs,' said Roy, after an awkward silence. 'They're pretty strict.'

'Six months at The Beeches. And how are you? *You?'*

'Fine.'

'You look after us all. Are we all looking after you?'

Roy had been cornered by the Chaplain before. He tried the usual response, 'I have everything I need?' but realised it shouldn't have sounded like a question. The Chaplain smiled and leaned back into his chair.

'Let's think about that together.'

The Chaplain's soporific ramblings made Roy late for the drug collection. Speeding across town, he reached the Memorial Hospital pharmacy ten minutes before they closed. As he loaded the padlocked chest onto the minibus, he spotted the elfin woman walking along a hospital corridor. He felt certain that it was *her* - the young woman who wore an ivory rose in the registrar's office: the bride to be. He hurried back into the building to search the corridors and waiting areas, but she was gone.

Roy liked the smell of the town library, with its smoky vanilla notes and a hint of floor polish. He usually arrived early each week to explore the shelves. This evening, there was no time to browse. In a windowless study room, he joined eleven other students, who were quietly absorbed in a reading task. Quite a few people read their 'happy day' text aloud. The tutor sat with Roy after the session.

'Is everything well at the moment, Roy?'

Roy couldn't resist smiling. Why did everyone seem to be asking him the same question? He was happy, wasn't he? He had everything he needed. Thinking of the care home had made him realise how much better things were nowadays.

'Everything's fine.'

'Our class is about more than pen and paper. It's important for us to understand the *power* of words ... of our language.'

'Was it no good?'

'I wouldn't say that. I would suggest that your piece was ... a little too revealing. Whatever we say or write about, it's often best to hold back the most personal details of one's life – to recognise those boundaries.'

'Is that like discreet?'

'Exactly, Roy. I remember we looked it up in the dictionary.' The tutor smiled back, pleased that her advice had been understood. Roy felt comforted by the middle-age woman. He could easily imagine her as his own mother: friendly and kind, her colourful handknitted sweater the product of a more settled life. 'One small example. If Juliet really was your girlfriend's name ...'

'It was.'

'Then use a different name. It's a simple way of protecting her identity.'

'Julia. Like Julia?'

‘Or alter it even more.’

Roy rode slowly along the promenade. The longest day of the year had passed. Holidaymakers were out for their evening walk, enjoying the crazy antics of starlings in the cloudless sky. Back in his bedsit, he sifted through the ingredients inside a bruised supermarket sandwich and sorted through his clean laundry, each item immaculately folded. He felt lagged by the day’s unusually early start, but he neatly wrote a new draft of his ‘happy day’ writing activity - *It all started with Jennifer ...*

*

Friday brought searing heat. Before setting off for his patients, Roy spent minutes trying to persuade the carpark cat to leave the shade of the minibus. A red van approached and parked alongside. The corpulent driver emerged, donning his peak cap and sunglasses.

‘What’s up, mate? Car trouble?’

‘It’s a cat. I can’t get him to move.’

The driver took a length of metal ducting from his van and poked it energetically under the vehicle. The terrified animal fled.

'You need to show him who's boss.' The engineer gestured to the new adhesive signage on his old van. Norton Commercial Heating. I'm my own boss. Where will I find the facilities manager? Angela what's her name?'

'Agnieszka - The facilities room. I'll show you.'

Norton held up an arresting hand.

'No problem, mate. I'll get a tea first.'

The ex-policeman had been waiting on his garden path for almost an hour. His wife gave a relieved smile, folded her umbrella and turned back to the house in tears.

'I thought you'd forgotten me, young man,' the patient complained. Roy was bang on time, as always. This comedy sketch had the same script every week. 'I know you, don't I?'

The tail lift wheezed and stuttered. The frightened man hung on to his wheelchair for dear life.

'Roy Birch! ... no previous convictions.' Roy secured the chair and fastened the tail lift. 'Where are we going?' asked the policeman, in a more conciliatory tone.

'The Beeches, but first, we're going to pick up your friends.'

'I don't have any friends.'

'Frances Dyer? She used to be an actress?'

Roy drove to Rose Gardens. The manicured cul-de-sac was a blaze of colour; the high summer heat had produced an abundance of blooms in every garden. Frances was standing at her gate, wearing her black cape. She cradled a small bunch of long stem roses, as if they were a baby. Roy lowered the step with a slightly theatrical gesture. Walking to her usual seat at the rear, Frances paused to hand the policeman a rose. Roy's mind wandered, as he weaved through neighbouring roads for his regulars. The addled ex-policeman's memory had exhumed an uncomfortable memory of his own - his best kept secret. He selected a country music disc and played a couple of songs to reinter the intrusive thoughts.

Since his arrival at the hospice, the driver of the red van had spent most of the time in the refectory, blagging a full English and numerous refills of tea. Norton had only bled a few radiators on the ground floor and created a puddle of rusty water for Roy to mop up.

'No, they're not working, observed the engineer. Let's get to the heart.'

'Careful on the last few steps. The edging is coming loose,' advised Roy.

'You want to fix that,' declared Norton, hauling his large case of tools and a rucksack into the roof space. Their voices echoed around the bare-brick landing and moss-covered skylight window.

Norton followed Roy along the dark corridor and through a couple of service doors. He switched on some bright maintenance lamps, to reveal a huge water tank and a maze of pipes. Some of the lagging hung down, like shed snakeskin.

'Guess you don't come up here much.'

'It's not part of my job.'

'Until today, eh?'

Norton located the gurgling gas boiler and opened its thin metal door with a flourish. He looked at the flickering control panels with a mixture of disappointment and contempt. He took a powerful torch from his rucksack and scanned the adjacent pipes.

'No wonder. I haven't seen a Genesis III for five years ... still working, that is.' He placed an ear against the outer casing. 'You've got air in the system.'

'Is that why it switches itself off?'

'Could be. Could well be. We'll have to see. This is a process. You start at the head, listen to the heart, and work yourself down to the belly of the beast.'

Norton shone his torch at the pipework and followed it back to the water tank. He thumped the tank with his fist. An impressive booming sound took seconds to die.

'At least we know the tank is full.' He banged the tank again, delighted by the thunderous sound. 'I'll make a start. I expect you've got a lot to do.'

'My line manager said you're welcome to a tea or coffee in the refectory.

'Did he?'

'She.'

'Very kind. I've got your number. I'll let you know if I need anything.'

Roy turned to leave. 'Oh, you'll hear the fire alarm. It's just a test.'

Norton shone the torch under his chin, to look sinister.

'You hope.'

With no other morning chores, Roy swabbed the mortuary and ate his fish and chips in peace. He watched a couple of nurses, looking intently at their smartphones. Agency staff came and went. There were new faces every few weeks and, not understanding their languages, he rarely spoke to them. When a contracted employee left, the whole building went in to mourning. Roy had to sign oversized leaving cards and join everyone for oversized slices of oversweet cake.

'Close the door.' Mrs King only made this request when she needed to be discreet. Roy sat and leaned forward. 'Roy, it's your first Open Day on Sunday. We all need to make a good impression and I'm sure you will.' She carefully placed some banknotes on the desk. 'I've added enough for you to get a haircut.'

'From my savings?

'Yes, it's a personal expense.'

'Will I get paid for coming in on Sunday?'

'A day in lieu. It goes towards your holiday allowance. See your contract of employment for the terms.'

Roy didn't understand Mrs King's answer. He decided to take his mysterious contract to the next literacy lesson and ask his tutor to decipher it.

'Is there anything else?'

'Something I was meaning to ask. I want to get a fridge for my place. A small one, for milk.'

'I can't imagine you have the space such a thing.'

'Very small ...'

'Or the need, to be frank. This heatwave will be over in a few days' time. Speaking of heat, when can we expect to have hot water?'

'The engineer doesn't know yet. He said it's a process.'

'Make sure he doesn't leave before it's fixed. Open Day without hot water ... can you imagine?'

Roy pocketed the banknotes and walked slowly up the service stairs. He passed the noisy boiler. Some of its electronic entrails were lying on the floor, still connected by a ganglion of coloured wires. Two more doors took him out on to the flat roof. He instantly felt the rising heat. Norton was leaning back in a chair borrowed from the refectory. With his boiler suit tied at the waist, the large, pale man displayed numerous tattoos. Each arm was covered in intricate images that continued to his neck. Norton opened one eye.

'What time is it, mate?'

Roy opened his clamshell phone. 'Two-thirty.'

'Said the man to the dentist.'

'Dentist?'

Norton shaded his eyes and studied Roy carefully. 'It's nothing. You're all right, mate.'

'Mrs King wants hot water.'

'Or I'll be in it. Tell her it'll be done. It's the solenoid. I've got one on the van.'

'Great. I'll let her know.'

Norton stood and stretched. He tried to lift the chair, but it was firmly embedded in the melted asphalt.

'I'll have to leave that for you.'

At going home time, the day centre procession began. Roy wheeled the policeman to the baking minibus, with the other regulars in his wake. Frances was still trying to give away her roses, but most flowers wilted on the empty passenger seats. When the wheelchair was gone, the remaining passengers requested, as they always did, to be taken home next. Only Frances remained silent, draining the contents of her hip flask. In Rose Gardens, Frances' foot faltered on the vehicle step. Roy held her securely while she regained her balance.

I don't know if I can go on, she declared quietly. He could smell the bourbon on her breath. I think you'll have to carry me. Sweeping her up in her arms with ease, he carried his passenger along the winding path.

'My ferryman. My leading man,' she muttered. 'The door is open.' Roy carefully placed her on a chair in the cool hallway. 'We're across the threshold, my dear. You'll have to excuse me, it's the medicine.'

'Should I call a doctor?'

'No, no.' Roy stood to one side and waited quietly. Frances stood. 'Better, now. Strange, the way it comes and goes. Let me show you something.'

She led him along a corridor lined with dozens of showbiz photographs - into the dining room, where some sunlight managed to filter through a gap in the heavy curtains. Frances switched on two glowing pendant lights, to reveal a coffin, resting on a makeshift bier. Every inch of the casket was brightly painted – a richly patterned floral design.

'You'll notice that I included a few thorns. Life wasn't all a bed of roses. What do you think?'

'You did this? He replied, admiringly.'

'All of it.'

'It's beautiful. He touched the coffin in a couple of places. Roses and azaleas.'

'Careful, it's still drying.'

'Wow.'

'Will you be there, Roy? On the day?'

He was caught off-guard. Although he'd transported floral arrangements to dozes of cremations and burials, he'd never been invited to a funeral service before today.

'Is that an invitation?'

'You don't need an invitation to attend someone's funeral. It's the law.'

Roy wished he'd known that before now. He had been fond of many patients. He would like to have attended their services.

'Of course. Who else will be there?'

‘That’s a very interesting question. I’ll never know the answer.’ They listened to the mantel clock counting the seconds. ‘I’ll see you next Friday,’ Frances promised. As the front door closed, she removed her blonde wig.

CHAPTER FIVE

The hospice had a rent-free charity shop in town. Its location near the supermarket ensured a steady stream of bargain hunters. Now in her second year of widowhood, Carole ruled a small army of volunteers, who sorted through a dozen bin bags of clothing and bric-a-brac left in the doorway every day. Staff occasionally fought over high-end handbags and fashion shoes, but the stock was mostly serviceable high street garments. The remaining rags were loaded on to the minibus for recycling. Roy got first dibs on books, but there were always too many to look through. Today, he settled on a handsome tome - 'Birds of South America'.

'I've got just the thing for you.' Carole rifled through a rack of men's clothing and extracted a leather motorcycle jacket, its embroidered skull patches scuffed and torn. 'Perhaps not.'

'Do you have a suit? Ordinary? Dark?'

‘Always.’ She quickly selected three suits and held a charcoal grey jacket against his chest. ‘I’ll need to lengthen the sleeves. ‘You’re not leaving us, are you?’ She added, genuinely concerned.

‘It’s for funerals.’

Roy parked the minibus and watched the arrival of an ambulance at the hospice entrance. Three or four patients made their final journey every week – some ambulant, but most in a wheelchair, their heads bowed through weakness and resignation. Today it was a short man in his twenties, wearing a brightly-coloured holiday shirt and sunglasses. Roy was intrigued to see someone his own age. He was obviously watching too intently, because the short man smiled and gave a cheerful wave. How differently every patient reacted to their approaching end. Acceptance was usually the way to go, but a significant few were determined to achieve some form of lastminute reprieve with mindfulness and complementary therapies: vitamins, herbs, tinctures and copper bracelets. For some, The Lord’s wish to ‘take them home’ was the only medicine they needed. The supernatural played a big role with its promise of being reunited with loved ones; 'crossing over,' 'passing on' and 'stepping into the next room' was not the end, but a new beginning. For a select few it was the promise of absolutely nothing: to be insensate; to surrender a lifetime of experiences and sensations to oblivion. Was this the most terrifying thought, or the most comforting?

Roy snapped back to the present. He realised that Norton's red van was gone. Washing his hands with hot water, he discovered this was good news. A quick scan of the wards was his last duty; a broken trolley and two bulb replacements were soon fixed. As he left the building, he looked over his shoulder to the upper storey windows, half expecting to see the 'ghost of Side Room Six'.

Roy cycled to the end of the pier and stared out across the motionless sea. The voices and laughter of passers-by carried easily on the still, evening air. The tide was as high as he'd ever seen it. He watched a glittering shoal of fish tug at weed on the submerged iron supports. On perfect evenings like this, he thought how good it would be to share his life with someone. Juliet had been in his mind. Would it be wrong to try and find her? Agnieszka would show him how to search on the internet. The idea soon dissolved. Mrs King had advised him to steer clear of past associations – the 'bad elements out to take advantage of him'. He rode back and forth along the seafront, until his body ached. When Roy hit the freshly-laundered pillow that night, he went out like a light.

*

The first Saturday cremation was at ten-forty. Roy parked the florist van behind the crematorium and placed Gina's handiwork alongside some bunches of flowers: *Rest in peace; Always in our hearts; Until we meet again.* Roy had seen all the handwritten dedications before. *Heaven couldn't wait* was taped to a small teddy bear. He had nowhere else to be, so he moved into the shade of a tree and watched the mourners assembling. The rear door of a shining hearse opened with unnatural slowness. Pallbearers moved in to position with pleasing symmetry and extracted a white coffin, barely a metre in length. The tight-knit cortège looked almost comical; four men were overkill for this small casket. Roy followed the mourners to the entrance and watched proceedings from the doorway. The celebrant's speech was too quiet to hear clearly. When a Disney song played on the loudspeakers, Roy left and followed a path to the centre of the cemetery. He read a few epitaphs aloud, wiping lichen from a couple of obscured words. *Memento Mori* made it into his notebook; his tutor would help him with that one.

'Enjoying the weather?' The barber asked brightly. Roy sat rigidly in the pneumatic chair. His haircut looked nothing like the chosen photograph. 'It grows back,' he reminded himself. The barber positioned a mirror to display a thick band of pale skin across Roy's neck. He managed a nod of approval.

Open Day was a great success. Mrs King was in her element, hosting the annual fundraising event with two new major sponsors. The mayor, nursing staff and patients applauded her speech about the importance of palliative care. They then listened politely to equally long speeches about the importance of home insulation and personal insurance. Roy helped Bernice and the kitchen staff distribute snacks. He avoided small talk with any of the visitors and found himself a couple of cleaning jobs on the wards to escape. A familiar wave drew his attention – the smiling young man, his complexion as drab as the gown he was now wearing.

'I saw you on Friday. You're the driver?'

'And facilities assistant,' answered Roy.

'I swear I recognise you.'

Roy instinctively looked away; introductions like this usually didn't end well.

'St. John's?' Roy nodded slowly. 'Thought so. You were in the year above me. You left early, right?'

'Sort of.'

'I think you were the tallest kid in the school. Roy ... ?'

'Roy Birch.'

'That's it. Michael Pappas. And we've ended up in the same place. I think that's like a sign ... I like that.' A few more names were exchanged. Previously demonised teachers were remembered with affection.

'Can I get you anything else, Michael?'

'Mike ... your friend for life.'

Roy spent the rest of his day leaning against a beach wall, trying to break his stone-throwing record. He took a foil-clad brick of leftover hospice sandwiches from his backpack and treated dozens of shrieking seagulls. With the grub gone, the birds gave him the evil eye and went off to torment a beach barbecue. The lowering sun set the sky on fire. When Roy began to ride, he discovered one of his tyres was punctured. He cut through the fairground, where roustabouts were securing thick tarpaulins over the rides; they knew as much about weather as the birds. The sound of thunder quickened Roy's pace. He carried his bust bike through the narrowest of passageways, reaching home minutes before the deluge.

*

The dawn ushered in a new week. Roy rode along steaming pavements, weaving between cars that were stranded on flooded side roads. Agnieszka was off sick, so the usual Monday disarray was even more challenging. The most important task was mopping up one end of the ward, where rain had dripped through the ceiling overnight, followed by the mortuary, where the Reddington crew waited patiently. One of the undertakers read the wrist tag to confirm name of the deceased - Gordon H. Marsh; acute myelomonocytic leukaemia with eosinophilia; pacemaker; one set prosthetic teeth. He and his colleague respectfully transferred the body. He handed Roy some pound coins and wheeled away his charge. Before leaving the room, Roy checked the refrigerator shelves. Only two of the twelve spaces were occupied, but one body had been there for more than a week. He twisted the wrist tag until he could read the barely-legible woman's name. He couldn't remember the face. Perhaps she was one of the patients who died hours after their arrival, or perhaps death had transformed her beyond recognition. Roy dropped the coins into Agnieszka's gratuities jar and polished off the last of her biscuits. Unable to find the body release form in his tray, he went through Agnieszka's papers, where he discovered a police incident form. He saw 'crime number' and a couple of words in the description – 'assault, bodily', before carefully returning the form to its original position. Roy returned to his desk and stared at Agnieszka's empty chair, unsettled. He considered reading the form, but knew that he'd give himself away; he'd reveal something in conversation; it wasn't his business: leave it. He replaced the empty oxygen cylinders, swapped the full sharps boxes, loaded salt into the softener and wrestled with a pile of overfilled refuse bags. The overnight rain had saved him one task – the minibus was gleaming.

After driving his regulars to the day centre, Roy was cornered by Grace, one of the senior volunteers.

'Roy, dear ... how are you?'

'Good.' After an awkward silence, he tried a new tactic. 'You?'

'Splendid. Tell me something, have you ever seen my newsletter?' Grace unfolded a home-made flyer, with a bright yellow banner. 'The Light.'

'I haven't. What's it about?'

'The afterlife. A guide to the seven psychic secrets. It brings such comfort, knowing that we'll be reunited with those we love.'

'This is for the patients?'

'For everyone. I printed fifty copies last week and they've all gone.'

'That's good, isn't it.' Roy leaned back to press the lift button.

'It's not good. I left some at reception, in the day room and the prayer room. Someone's taken them all. And it's not the first time. Would you happen to know anything about this?'

'Nothing.'

'If you discover who is taking them, I'd like you to report it to me.'

Roy nodded earnestly and stepped backwards into the lift. He knew exactly where the flyers had gone. While guests were sunning themselves on Open Day, the Chaplain had located every copy of The Light and disposed of them: this was a competition for souls. Roy knew he shouldn't get involved.

Lunch was equally uncomfortable. After an hour in the warming cabinet, Roy's grey slices of meat and gravy had lost their charm. He was about to abandon the congealed mess when Bernice parked herself firmly on the facing seat.

'Where did you go yesterday afternoon? You disappeared.'

'I had a few things to do on the ward,' he replied.

'You weren't avoiding me, then?' Roy felt Bernice's broad, kitchen-hot hand grip his knee. This was a new development, for which he was unprepared. He felt obliged to swallow a few unpleasant mouthfuls. 'I could tell you everything you need to know about bodybuilding.' She gave his thigh a good squeeze. 'Given any thought to my proposal?' Roy smiled weakly, quite out of his depth. 'Wrestling.'

'Oh, right. I don't think I'd be much of a fighter.'

'It's not fighting. Anyway, you should let me be the judge of that. I'll teach you a few moves.' Bernice leaned forward and lowered her voice. 'A few of the basic holds.'

'Thank you, Bernice.'

'You're the best. I could eat you.' The muscle-bound cook winked and launched herself back towards her domain.

Now the fundraising memorial benches were dry, Roy could return them to the dim, damp hospice basement. He put his feet up. This would be a good place to lie low for a while: perhaps close his eyes until the patients' going home time. Rossini roused him after a few drowsy minutes; he was wanted on the ward. Michael's condition had deteriorated overnight and he was being transferred to Side Room Two for privacy. Roy rolled the furniture and accompanying medical paraphernalia into the hot, airless room.

'Number two ... my lucky number, Michael announced cheerfully. You see, I always land on my feet.' Roy re-connected all the cables and restored a Mad Max episode to Michael's monitor. 'Hope I live long enough to find out how the movie ends.' Michael put a silencing finger to his lips. 'No spoilers.'

'I haven't seen it,' Roy replied.

'So, where did you go after St. John's?'

'I went away.' Roy managed to force open the window a few inches. He closed his eyes against the cooling breeze.

'I couldn't get away. My old mum's a widow. Doesn't speak a word of English. What could I do? Parcel delivery was the perfect job. I could always swing by during the day if she needed me ... quite often, as it turned out.' Roy pulled up a chair, strangely comforted by his schoolfriend's acceptance. 'Lost the job, of course. Being stuck at home almost killed me.'

Mrs King hovered in the doorway. 'Roy ... a word, please.'

Sotto voce in Side Room Three, the hospice manager explained that they had 'a situation'. There'd been a development on the 'long-term mortuary occupant'. The deceased's siblings – two brothers – had fought over the choice of undertaker. One of them was seriously injured and 'is currently in hospital'. The other brother was threatening to visit the hospice to 'see his beloved sister'.

'I've explained this to Val ...'

'Who's Val?'

'Our new receptionist. She's to call the police if he shows up ... and I want you standing guard. I don't want him in the building.'

'What about the patients?'

'Of course ... this is before and after your daily run.'

Roy remembered the name on the wristband. 'Brierly?'

'Graham Brierly,' she confirmed and touched Roy's arm in a half-hearted gesture of trust. 'I'll be in my office if you need me.'

Roy sauntered down the service stairs, wondering what had got into everyone today: what a time for Agnieszka to be away. He spent the next twenty minutes comforting the frail-looking receptionist, who was in tears. She had wanted to work here because it was 'the most peaceful place' she could find. He knew Val would be gone by the end of the week. There'd be no oversized leaving card, or even a small one.

After taking the patients home, Roy returned to a seat at the back of reception, partially concealed behind a yellowing and root-rotting yucca. Overwatered by every considerate receptionist, the huge plant was now bending over at an acute angle. When Val checked her wristwatch for the sixth time, Roy suggested she leave. He also reassured Mrs King, who phoned from her office every twenty minutes. His mind wandered as shafts of early evening sunlight cast forensic rays across the desk and seating area. For the first time, he noticed how tatty the furniture looked. The cheap desk was missing thin strips of veneer and the chair stuffing had perished, with shiny scars on the worn headrest. It had looked so smart in February, when he arrived for his interview. He felt at home. It was the knackered stuff he was so familiar with from the children's home and the young offender institution. Kicking off his charity shop boots, he considered the transience of life. One hour later, he was awakened by a loud bang. Crossing to the main door, he discovered a large blackbird that had flown in to the glass and left its ghostly imprint. He carefully transferred the unconscious animal to a sheltered spot in the reception area. He looked closely at its translucent eyelids and pulsing chest. If this was curtains for the creature, it was certainly in the right place. An idle search through the reception desk yielded a pencil sharpener, an empty stapler and a glass marble. In the bottom drawer, Roy discovered a crumpled copy of The Light; this would engage him for the rest of the evening. The flyer informed him that the phenomena of Nature, both physical and spiritual, are the expression of Infinite Intelligence and that life continues after death. He couldn't understand why the Chaplain took exception to these ideas. It sounded like the same religious stuff that various guardians and wardens had tried to drum into his head over the years. A scratching sound drew his attention to the blackbird that was now standing on the doormat, resurrected. Roy slowly opened the door and watched it fly away. He decided not to tell Agnieszka about this; she'd surely see it as an omen. The hospice exterior lights flickered in to life as a couple of the night staff parked their cars. Roy called it a day.

CHAPTER SIX

'Morning, Angie.' There was slight trepidation in Roy's greeting.

'You're a sight for sore eyes,' she smiled. How did it go yesterday?

'Easy, it was fine. I can hold the fort ... if you need more time.'

Roy and Agnieszka stared at each other, uncomfortably. She removed her dark glasses. 'It's all right, I haven't been hit again. I just have a headache. By the way, I know you've been through my filing.'

Roy feigned innocence, then grimaced. 'Yes, but I didn't see anything ... not really.'

'Oh, Roy ... you are sweet. You were looking for the Brierly release form. I've put it in your tray. The undertakers are here at ten.'

Roy unfolded the form and struggled with the text. 'Squamous cell carcinoma of supraglottic larynx. Who understands this stuff?'

'Educated people. Mrs King was impressed with you. Standing guard yesterday. She wants me to educate you. Train you up, I think she said. How can I do that if you can't read English?'

'I can read,' he protested.

'Here, pull up your chair.' Agnieszka prised the cover off a syringe driver. 'I'm going to show my apprentice how to do something useful. We're going to clean and recalibrate the mechanism. We're not meant to do this ...'

'We're not authorised.'

'Correct, but if it goes back to the hospital for maintenance, we'll never see it again. And, do help yourself to one of my biscuits.'

She gestured to her empty biscuit tin. Roy returned Agnieszka friendly grin, relieved to see her in a good mood. 'Is there anything I can do to help you?' He gestured to her bruised face.

'It's over. He's gone back to Poland.'

'Your husband?'

'God, no ... who would get married.' Agnieszka spat out a few words in Polish, then took a deep breath. 'My husband was even worse.'

A crew from City Funeral Directors arrived early. The two women waited patiently in reception until Roy arrived. He was impressed by their matching suits and smart blouses. Company badges displayed their names. The late Mrs Brierly was soon transferred to her temporary coffin and good to go. The older undertaker opened her wallet.

'Out of interest, who gets most of your business? Which funeral directors?'

'It's usually Reddington. They're local.'

The women exchanged a quick look. The older woman placed a banknote into Roy's hand and closed his fingers around it. He was slightly confused. He felt he should offer some change.

'Thank you, Roy, I'm sure we'll meet again.'

The younger undertaker turned and moved unusually close to Roy. She reached into her jacket and presented her business card. 'My name's Holly. I'm fairly new to the business, but I'm getting the hang of it.' She smiled and pushed a lock of wayward hair behind her ear. 'Bye.'

Agnieszka was similarly impressed by the woman's largesse: enough for a few packs of calming cigarettes and comforting biscuits. City Funeral Directors & Co was now bound to come up in any conversations with the patients and relatives.

Two Wednesday patients had become good friends. The women's recollections and laughter made the journey around the town and country roads a relaxing tour. They teased-out all the threads of their lives – the places frequented and the friends they once had in common – amazed that they hadn't met before now. Today, their chief concern was the fate of their dogs. Roy was unable to accept the offer of a 'loving, spayed, two-year-old King Charles Spaniel' or an 'arthritic Labrador'. He explained that he wasn't allowed pets in his bedsit, or visitors after ten o'clock.

Roy's curry lunch was mercifully uninterrupted. He stopped at the laundry doorway to greet the Marias, then checked on ward repairs. He was careful not to wake Michael and his mother in Side Room Two. The exceptionally short woman was perched on a visitor chair, her stockinged feet well above the floor. Dressed entirely in black, it looked as if she was already in mourning. A bead rosary was wound around her child-size fist like a knuckleduster.

Roy's vibrating mobile phone told him it was already going home time. He reversed the minibus to the entrance door, thoroughly checked all seats and belts and returned his passengers to their loved ones. Arriving back at the hospice, Roy was disappointed to find Norton's red van hogging his favourite spot in the car park. He glanced through the open driver's window - at a mountain of receipts and fast-food wrappers strewn across the dashboard. A pink, silk baby bootie was hanging from the rearview mirror. Agnieszka wanted nothing to do with this man; this would be an assignment for her apprentice.

Head bowed in the roof space, Roy shone his torchlight between the rafters and cascading pipe insulation. He stepped over the Genesis boiler access panel and its eviscerated wiring. He found Norton slumped in the immovable roof chair.

'Turns out it wasn't the solenoid,' Norton stated confidently.

'No?'

'Of course, it doesn't have to be just one thing. Once one thing goes ...' Norton took the last bite out of an apple and hurled the core over the edge of the roof. Roy heard it land in the carpark. He knew he'd be picking that up later, if the rats didn't find it first. 'It's like a chain reaction. Nothing lasts,' he pronounced with a sigh.

'Will we get hot water today? enquired Roy. Everyone's upset.'

Norton sat back in the seat and gazed solemnly into the distance. 'Everything can be fixed, can't it? If I didn't believe that, I wouldn't be here.' Roy nodded very slowly, unsure if the question was rhetorical. 'If we order new circuit boards today ...' Norton flicked each of his fingers out, until his hand was flat. 'Friday week ... or the Monday after ... at the latest. I can keep it working until then.' Norton turned his face back to the sun. 'I'm running tests.'

As Roy retraced his steps through the roof spaces, a bright crimson reflection caught his eye – the lining of a sleeping bag, half-concealed behind a roof partition. Plastic food boxes and jam jars were also carefully tucked out of sight. Was Norton expecting to camp here? It would be easy to escape evasion. Roy decided to keep this to himself. Agnieszka would surely send the man on his way and the water problem would be made worse. Within an hour, steam was rising from the hospice showers and order had been restored. It merited an approving pat on the back from Agnieszka. With no budget for a new boiler, the cost of a few spare parts was easy to swallow. She guided Roy through the ordering process and showed him how to file the associated invoices on the spreadsheet. All in all, it had been a productive day: going home time. He couldn't resist racing his bike along the empty promenade and skidding through a slalom of bollards.

Public donations were always welcome. Most items went directly to the charity shop in town, but the booze always came directly to the hospice reception. Spirits and liquors were the lifeblood. Cupboards of the deceased and their relatives produced dozens of bottles every month. Mrs King had one rule: none would be accepted if the seal had been broken. Roy was given the task of pouring the contents of opened bottles down the sink. What she didn't know was that most rejected alcohol ended up in Agnieszka's private cupboard in the facilities room. The drinks would range from fine malts all the way down to ouzo and advocaat – regretted airport purchases. As Roy wheeled his bike through reception on Thursday morning, he caught Agnieszka checking all the seals in a case of claret. She waved a distracting hand towards a dozen black bin bags and stuffed backpacks. After the morning passenger run, Roy took the donated clothes to the charity shop. They were delighted with the haul. The plus size rail was most popular with the townswomen and today it would groan under the weight.

'Lots of these have never been worn, remarked Grace.'

'As new,' echoed the fellow volunteer.

Grace hurried through a bead curtain and returned with Roy's 'new' suit. She'd lengthened the sleeves and was pleased with the tailored fit. 'It gives you gravitas,' she commented. 'Clothes maketh the man,' added the fellow volunteer.

'That's quite a haircut,' said Carole, reaching up to stroke Roy's number three. 'Makes you look older. Now, if I was twenty years younger ...'

Roy hung his suit on a passenger seat and secured it with the seat belt. He made it to The Memorial Hospital pharmacy in good time and signed for the controlled drugs. As he lifted the padlocked chest into the minibus, he heard an unsettling voice directly behind.

'Looks like a pirate chest. What have you got in there? Treasure?' The youth was more subdued today, with two wing plasters holding his cheek together.

'Beano?'

'Good memory.'

You here for treatment?' asked Roy, indicating the face wound.

'No. They ask too many questions. Never a good idea.'

'If it needs cleaning ...' Roy's half-finished thought faded away. He locked the vehicle, as Beano circled, looking through each of the windows.

'This where you work then? ... at the hospital?'

'No.'

'So where do you work?'

'It's a private place.' Roy's delayed reply almost sounded like a question.

'Good answer. I like that. What use is anyone if they can't keep a secret?' In one swift and easy movement, Beano raised his phone to take a photograph. 'For the record, Roy.' Beano's slow and deliberate response sounded like a threat. Roy took his seat behind the wheel and pulled away. He glanced at Beano's resolute figure in the rear-view mirror. He paused on the seafront road to make a note of his encounters with Napoleon and his loony lieutenant, together with the dates and times. He learned at a young age that it helps to keep one's own record of events. 'One never knows,' as his probation officer used to say.

Roy's pizza lunch was larger than usual, with tiers of added ingredients. A yellow Post-it note stuck to the edge of the plate made him smile: Rebel Roy. He wolfed the lot; Bernice would be impressed. After going home time, he collected half a pallet of outdated donated food from the supermarket and worked through his remaining daily tasks: cleaning, waste, oxygen, domestic supplies and minor repairs. He made sure he had time to sit with his old schoolfriend Michael, before cycling to the library. The evening literacy session dragged; words blurred and the tutor's voice drifted. The coming week's task was to write a letter. He was to consider the format, the register and the salutations. Roy was puzzled. He'd never written a letter in his life and didn't know where to start. Lying in bed that night, he settled the pen in his left hand

and carefully formed each letter in his notebook, 'Dear Mother'.

CHAPTER SEVEN

Frances was unable to keep her promise. The actor had been on the Friday passenger list for almost five months, but today the show could not go on; she phoned in sick. Roy collected the rest of his regulars. The ex-policeman was unshaven, dishevelled and silent. The man's wife was eager to explain that he'd woken up in a 'strange room, with an unknown woman'. 'I'm at my wits end,' she stated quietly, through her teeth. 'Forgive me.'

The carpark cat was playing dead, stretched out on a particularly warm spot near the main entrance. Roy sounded the horn and slowly manoeuvred the minibus around the luxuriating creature. It yawned, wandered off and squeezed through a hedge.

'That's unlucky,' said one passenger disquietingly. 'It's an omen.'

'Oh, for heaven's sake,' sighed another.

'There's no need for that.'

‘Last week it was a bird on the windowsill ... and before that it was some flickering lights.’

‘Yes, one day before Alison passed away.’

The tiff continued quietly as Roy steered his patients into the building. Emerging from the lift, the group fell silent. Everyone tried to make sense of a new sound that rippled along the corridor: a low groan filled with dread. The patients were spirited away by concerned volunteers, as Roy continued to the wards and approached the source of the disquieting noise; it was Side Room Two. Mrs Pappas was teetering on the edge of Michael’s bed, like a midnight black succubus, tightly holding her son. Sister Nielsen and two nurses were gently trying to prise the woman from the dead body. The moan turned in to a wail. Mrs King arrived to console the woman, but to no effect. Suddenly, Mrs Pappas turned from the bed and threw her arms around Roy. Every person in the crowded room stood stock-still, as the wailing subsided and the crying began. A few minutes passed, before Mrs King felt able to steer Roy and the grieving mother back to the lift. In the car park, the exhausted woman released her limpet grip and collapsed into the seat of a relative’s car.

Going home time was a subdued affair. The superstitious patient wore her 'what did I tell you' expression in silence. For the rest of the day, the hospice was unusually quiet – regaining its composure after the traumatic morning. Roy cleared and cleaned Side Room Two for its next occupant. He disposed of the day's waste and sat silently by the bins, staring at the sunbathing cat. He'd been affected by Mrs Pappas' strength of feeling: how she must have loved her son. Roy tried to think about his own mother, but drew a blank. Did she ever hold him tightly or cry out for him? A long shadow reached the carpark cat. It rolled slowly backwards into the warm, late-afternoon light.

When Roy collected his neatly-folded clothes from the laundry, he was ambushed by the Marias who made him sit for a 'slide show' on their phones. A sister had just married in Manila. Dozens of wedding pictures were flicked through. Both devices finally settled on images of a smiling teenager, with flowers braided in her long dark hair. Through their chatter and laughter, Roy learned that this pretty woman was not the bride, but a niece ... waiting for her own wedding day. 'She will not wait long,' chorused the Marias. After a few questions about his income and residence, he realised he was being propositioned. 'She has excellent cooking and now she learns English,' came the reassurance. Roy nodded appreciatively. The women nodded back, giving him time to think about it.

In his bedsit, Roy unfolded his newly-pressed bedsheets. He discovered a laminated bookmark that had been tucked inside. The small gift featured a gilt-embossed Filipino blessing and a silken tassel. He placed it carefully on his shelf of favourite books and returned to the coming week's literacy letter task. His pen hovered above the words 'Dear Mother'. He tore the page out of his notebook.

A short shower did nothing to cool-off the sunbaked Saturday morning. Roy flicked the florist's delivery van through the cemetery gates with familiar ease and unloaded the floral tributes behind the cremation building. The largest wreath this week spelled out NAN in rosebuds with ivory lilies. The customer had wanted GRANNY, but their budget precluded. A fine arrangement of lilies was positioned for the eleven-twenty and a bouquet of gardenias for the twelve-forty.

'All right, Roy?'

He hadn't noticed the undertakers from Reddington, standing furtively behind a rhododendron bush. One was finishing a cigarette as his colleague peeled an orange.

'We haven't seen you for a while. Is no-one dying at The Beeches?'

'They're all dying,' Roy replied slowly.

'We're all dying, come to that,' sighed the second undertaker, as he tossed the orange peel into the bush. 'Food for the worms.'

'No-one's poaching our business, are they?'

Roy shrugged and turn to watch the mourners, who were carefully parking their cars in line and standing in solemn groups: the usual cast of characters for a regular performance. One of the mourners stood alone, facing away from the others. When the figure moved, Roy recognised the elfin woman; the bride-to-be he'd seen in the registration office ... and the person who darted along The Memorial Hospital corridor. He continued to watch the odd woman, as the mourners drifted into the crematorium building. He watched her sidle up to each of the mourners' cars and try the door handles. When one car door opened, the woman quickly reached inside and grabbed something to hide under her jacket.

'Hey ...' called Roy as he approached the cars. The woman pulled the hood of her jacket up and walked away, trying not to run. She was no match for Roy, who was at her side in seconds. The elfin woman leaned towards him, hissing like a scalded animal. She 'pointed' her jacket pocket at his chest.

'I'm not afraid to use it. It wouldn't be the first time.' They stood in silence: stalemate.

'I know you. I've seen you a few times.'

'Did they send you?' she asked, her voice wavering.

'Who?'

'Tell them to leave me alone. Just forget it.'

'What did you take from the car? I don't think it was yours.'

'Are you alone?' The elfin woman looked around nervously. 'If you follow me, I'll cut your face off.' The woman walked a few steps backwards, then turned and ran.

Roy hesitated. He could catch up with her, but what then? What would he say or do? The right thing would be to report what happened. He would wait until the service was over and tell the owner of the car what he'd witnessed. Roy didn't like the word 'witness' in his head. He could leave a note under the windscreen wiper. Did he know the right words? Perhaps she didn't take anything of value. The self-justification made him feel uneasy: easier to drive home. And anyway, there was no pen in the delivery van. He settled his conscience and drove from the cemetery, looking along the paths on either side of the narrow road. What had she meant by 'they,' and why was she so scared? Perhaps 'they' had ... who knows. By the afternoon, his concerns had percolated away. He sat on the Seashell Café terrace, holding his free coffee between two hands and watching the starlings, as they started their afternoon antics.

Roy's spending money just seem to disappear. After a few grocery items and a minor repair to his bike, he was spent. He had to buy his own food on the weekend. Every Sunday he knew the exact time that the two main supermarkets marked down outdated produce. He carried his haul up the bedsit stairs and watched the last rays of evening sun creep across the wall. He opened his clamshell work phone and scrolled through the patient contact numbers. It was time for a purge. He briefly created a mental picture of each deceased patient and erased their phone numbers. How many times had he done this before? The thought tired him. When he came to, the room was practically dark; night had crept up on him. As he replayed the day's events in his mind's eye, he suddenly sat bolt upright. 'It was her,' he whispered to the empty room; the elfin woman was the person in the hospice window: she was the ghost of Side Room Six.

Laughter and chatter from Gloria's bedroom continued in to the small hours. Roy stopped breathing momentarily to make out a few barely-intelligible words, then checked himself: none of his business - always best to keep out of other people's lives and not dwell on the past.

Michael Pappas' body was being collected at nine-thirty. Roy had enough time to spend a few minutes in the mortuary with his old schoolfriend. He kicked a wooden wedge into doorjamb – a habit he picked up from Agnieszka, who was frightened of being locked inside. Roy pulled on some gloves and pulled out the refrigerator trolley. With rigor mortis long gone, the corpse moved slightly as the trolley height was adjusted: for a second, the illusion of life. Michael looked smaller – as if he'd shrunk over the weekend. Attached to his gown was a small plastic bag, containing a dental plate with three prosthetic teeth. They would be returned to his mouth after embalming; his funeral was to be an open casket affair, with dozens of mourners. Michael would look his best. Roy stared at his friend's face, looking for any vestige of an earthly presence. Although he'd seen dozens of dead bodies before, this was the first time he truly understood the total absence. This shrinking shell was merely human remains. He found the realisation oddly reassuring. A loud ringtone released Roy from his reverie: the undertakers had arrived. When Roy dropped three one-pound coins into the facilities room jar, he noticed it was nearly empty. He knew where the money was going. Agnieszka always left enough to keep up the deception and he never mentioned it; it was their unspoken secret.

'Please close the door, Roy.'

Mrs King had 'two matters to discuss' - the first was an 'extremely sensitive issue'. Roy had to lean forward, in order to hear her voice. One of his patients would no longer be attending the day centre. The ex-policeman had been suffocated. His widow had been interviewed by the police for an hour and interviewed by the local newspaper for two hours. Their first feature would include photographs of the family home and an empty wheelchair. Mrs King said there would be rumours and that it was vital to keep any mention of The Beeches out of the news. On a lighter note, with a hint of a smile, she was pleased to inform Roy that he was in line for a pay rise in February. Her smile left as she went on to explain that it may have to be postponed for a further six months – the hospice's funds were in a parlous state. For this reason, the main ward was to lose two beds.

'What will happen to her?'

'Who?'

'The woman who killed her husband.'

Now, that is exactly the kind of rumour we need to avoid,' replied Mrs King. 'We must not assume anything. Can I be sure of your discretion?'

'Mum's the word.'

Roy dismantled two ancient, iron bedsteads and dumped them in the damp darkness of the basement storage, along with the forgotten benches of remembrance. He knew they would never be returned to the ward. They would rust away and eventually be taken away for scrap.

Roy climbed the last few stairs into the roof spaces and passed the boiler, that hummed quietly. Outside, on the roof, Norton was writing. The small, pink notebook with a star-spangled unicorn on its cover, looked incongruous in his huge hands.

'Belonged to my daughter. She doesn't need it anymore.'

'Oh, right ... OK,' said Roy, cautiously.

'Sorry to hear about your patient, mate.' Roy broke eye contact. 'The copper who copped it. Wife put him out of his misery?'

'Really? Where did you hear about this?'

'The cook. The dyke with black and white hair.'

'Dyke? What's that?'

'I think you've led a sheltered life. Am I right?'

Roy considered four replies, but decided to remain silent. Norton patted Roy gently on the back. 'You're all right. You're a good man.' He scrolled through a few pages on his phone and returned a unicorn pencil to the notebook's spine. 'This little book has saved me thousands of pounds. Take a look.' Norton slowly turned the pages. Every page was covered in columns of numbers. 'These are the winning lottery numbers for the last three years. And here ...' He flicked page to the first page. 'Here is the one set of numbers I chose back then.'

'You do The Lottery?'

Gambling's a mug's game. I never buy a ticket. I just compare the winning numbers with my number. It's never come up in three years. I'm the one that's laughing.'

'I guess so.'

'I know so. Mug's game.'

'The new parts for the boiler have been despatched. They could be here as early as tomorrow.' Norton looked disappointed. 'I haven't said anything ... about you sleeping up here. I expect the boiler will need monitoring for a while, once you've put the new bits in.'

'Precisely,' answered Norton, gratefully. 'Cheers, mate. I owe you one.'

Late in the afternoon, an ambulance crew wheeled Frances to the lift. Their laughter proved she'd lost none of her charm. What she had lost during the last week was a lot of weight and strength. Once she was ensconced in Side Room Three, she asked Roy to sit with her. The bravado and cheerfulness of their last meeting had left. The actor now looked unnerved, unsure of her lines. She removed her wig and unsecured her robe, to reveal a dark, glistening melanoma across her neck and chest.

'I can feel it now ... gnawing away. Perhaps you'll find me a hand mirror from somewhere. I haven't looked at myself for some time.' Her hands moved slowly downwards, revealing the diseased skin across her breasts. She stared in consternation, as if inspecting the invasion for the first time. Roy felt uncomfortable. He checked the corridor for any nursing staff and moved close to the door. 'Not exactly flattering are they, these ceiling lights,' she observed. Roy switched off the main light. The single bedside lamp transformed Frances in to a weathered marble bust: lichen on rock. 'Better. Much better,' she sighed.

'I'll find you a mirror.'

Roy saw curious eyes scanning the side room. It was the Chaplain, cruising the hospice wards, looking for souls to save. Roy closed the blind.

CHAPTER EIGHT

A Detective Chief Inspector was travelling from Birmingham to visit his sister – or rather her body. Roy had helped with two other viewing requests in the past, but this would be his first unaided. On his first day at the hospice, he'd asked about the pale green second door in the mortuary. It led to a small adjoining room that was strangely incongruous. The Victorian wallpaper, dado rails and dim, brass wall lights made it look like a museum tableau. Two bucolic Constable landscapes were as faded as their gilt frames; this was the viewing room. Roy extracted the woman's body from the refrigerator. He checked and double-checked the nametag and wheeled her carefully through the narrow doorway. He checked through the drawers of a small chest for items he'd need – a pillow, a musty bedspread and a hairbrush. He lifted each of her arms onto the bedspread and positioned her head on the pillow. Brushing her hair made all the difference; she no longer looked dead, but asleep. Spray from a can of air freshener was the finishing touch. Roy unlocked the second door, which opened directly on to the corridor. This is where the policeman would enter.

The Inspector was bang on time. He waited at reception, hat held tightly under one arm. Roy led the visitor along the ground floor corridor, slightly disconcerted by the man's uniform and the rhythmic echo of his steel-toed shoes. The Inspector hesitated at the open viewing room door.

'How much time do I have?'

'As much as you want. Come to the facilities room when you're through. It's the second door on the right.'

Roy put his feet up and stared at the blank page in his notebook. Who could he write a letter to? He could say what he wanted; no-one was going to read it. Michael? Frances? The policeman's sister? He felt oddly inspired. He could practise his skills by sending letters that would never be read. Twenty minutes later, Roy returned to the mortuary and looked through the green viewing room peephole. The man was bent over the woman's body, stroking each of her hands in turn. Roy continued to observe for a few minutes, then withdrew quietly. The mortuary was getting too warm, with refrigerator fans expelling heated air. He waited in the cooler corridor. Early evening was always the quietest time of the day, with the laundry closed and the nursing staff handover completed. After another twenty minutes, Roy peered into the viewing room. The man was slumped on one knee, his head resting on the bedspread. He remained stationary for a further five minutes, before standing and pulling his uniform straight. This was Roy's cue. He quickly returned to the corridor and met the grieving man.

'I understand you have a prayer room, with a book of condolences.' Roy locked the viewing room and led the Inspector to the lift. 'How long may I stay?'

'As long as you need' replied Roy. 'The main door is locked now. When you're through ...'

'The facilities room.'

When Roy returned the woman's body to her temporary tomb, he was intrigued to see that a gold ring had been placed on her left hand. It wasn't recorded on the inventory card; her brother must have brought it with him. After another forty minutes, Roy silently opened the prayer room door. The Inspector was leaning heavily on the lectern, still writing his condolences. He turned the page and continued without pause. It was starting to grow dark when The Inspector was finally ready to leave. Roy felt relieved. After a quick scan of the wards, he returned to the prayer room – curious to know what the Inspector had written. Light spilled under the door: an unintelligible voice from the room. Roy silently opened the door to see the Chaplain now bowed over the lectern. As his muttering continued, the man tore a page out of the condolences book and crushed the paper with great force, as if punishing the paper. The Chaplain eventually realised he was not alone.

'Enter, Roy.'

Calming himself and slowing his breathing, the Chaplain picked up a few sheets of mangled paper from the floor and smoothed them out on the lectern, almost apologetically.

'Filth. Shameful. Not fit for anyone's eyes.' Roy stood his ground and waited. 'I'm sure he would come to regret writing this ... I'm saving him the embarrassment ... and a police officer, too.' The Chaplain sat wearily and motioned to a facing chair. 'We have to be on our guard. Especially here at The Beeches, where people are leaving this world. They lose their sense of decorum. Do you know what decorum means?'

'No.'

'As I feared. The theatre woman in the side room ...'

'Frances Dyer?'

'You must give her her privacy. *You* will have to do that. She will have lost her sense. I've seen it again and again. It's also the morphine. It loosens one's ...' The Chaplain's voice trailed off. He stared at the blank wall. Roy watched the wall clock second hand rotate once, then stole from the room.

As Roy rode his bike along the hospice corridor and in to the night, he wondered if he was the only person to have noticed that the Chaplain was not exactly right in the head. He thought of discussing it with Mrs King, but she was not much of a listener; she just liked to say things. Anyway, it would all rebound, as confidences always had in the past. Religious types had been especially spiteful.

'As I live and breathe.'

Roy braked hard. Lost in thought, he'd almost cycled in to Napoleon, who was leaning against a lamppost. This was the kind of encounter Roy was keen to avoid; he'd cut through the Municipal Gardens without thinking. Napoleon's henchman Beano sprang from his arbour seat.

'It's reckless Roy.'

'I'm just riding home.'

'Of course. How have you been, friend?'

'I've been OK, Roy replied cautiously.'

The streetlight above their heads switched itself on.

'Look at that. Summer's nearly over,' observed Napoleon, with an affected note of sad regret.

'The evenings are drawing in,' crooned Beano, as he put a foot on the front tyre, to prevent escape.

'You know, you could do better than 'OK'.' Napoleon smiled and walked behind the bike to divide Roy's attention. 'I have a proposition. Something you can do after hours.'

'I have a class every Thursday evening, at the library.' Roy chastised himself as soon as the words had left his mouth. He needed to keep quiet – to concentrate.

'It's rewarding work ... and there's no training required.'

'I'm good.'

‘Perhaps ... but you must be curious. Do you know this town well?’

‘I was born here.’

Roy had no idea if that was true. Being found outside the town’s police station didn’t exactly qualify.

‘Then you’re just the fellow. I can see you’re eager to get home ...’

‘Near the cemetery,’ Beano recalled.

‘So, leave us with your phone number, and we’ll discuss details some other time.’ Cold light from Napoleon’s iPhone made his sallow face glow. ‘Zero.’

‘Zero seven something. Honestly, I’m really not ...’

‘I’ve started now. Zero seven.’

Roy found it difficult to resist polite requests; it was an automatic response. He gave his number. Within seconds, the work phone in his backpack started ringing.

‘Come away, come away with William Tell. Come away to the land he loved so well,’ chanted Beano.

Silence. Roy studied the two faces that were waiting for him to speak. Beano rubbed the scar on his face.

‘We’ll speak again soon,’ stated Napoleon, with a friendly-looking smile. Beano released the bike.

As he rode furiously, Roy admonished himself again. Why did he give in to other people so easily, when he knew it always led to no good? He would block Napoleon's number as soon as he got home. What good would that do? He could call from any number – and so could anyone else.

Sitting on the edge of his bed, Roy opened his phone slowly, as if it might explode. The last call read 'private number'- withheld. Maybe he should 'lose' the phone. He imagined hurling it into the sea. That would only land him in deeper water and draw suspicion. For what? He hadn't done anything, he reasoned: not yet. Roy realised why he was so tired; he hadn't eaten that day. He took a foil pack from his bag and briefly considered eating the congealed mass. He'd make do with the inscribed banana. Bernice had used a biro to write another wrestling name suggestion along the skin, 'Bruiser Roy'. He reached for a pen and inscribed his own suggestion, 'Reckless Roy'.

Mrs King inspected the hospice wards and day room every morning, visiting the patients and dealing with any overnight issues. Even Nurse Nielsen, who'd been giving orders to her nursing staff for the last two hours, followed the hospice manager and quietly noted instructions. Roy was dealing with an oxygen delivery, when his phone rang for the first time that day. He opened his phone with slight trepidation – Mrs King wanted to meet in the prayer room. Roy was a poor liar. The manager watched his expression carefully, as he ran his finger down the condolence book spine.

'I don't understand why this has happened,' he said truthfully. 'No-one in their right mind would destroy something so precious to everyone here.'

'Indeed,' replied Mrs King. 'The last entry we have is now two weeks old. Would you please glue the two pages together, so the damage is concealed. I'm greatly indebted to you, Roy. How is your training coming along? Agnieszka?'

'She's teaching me every day,' he lied.

Roy stood in the doorway of Side Room Three, chatting to Frances. Her hospice gown was drawn as low as it could be, while maintaining her decency. What she had been most anxious to conceal in the past, was now a truth displayed; this was her final role and she meant to wow her audience. Seated by the window, she turned the pages of a scrapbook filled with her old press cuttings.

''Francis Dyer's Titania was beyond compare. This fantastical Queen of the forest transported theatregoers to her magical realm'. Desmond Montague, The Bexley & Bromley Times. Dear Desmond. I wonder what he's doing now. He's in that magic realm, probably.'

'I'm sorry I never saw you doing your acting.'

'So am I, dear.' Frances closed her eyes and stroked her forehead. 'The Fairyland buys not the child of me. His mother was a vot'ress of my order, and in the spicèd Indian air by night, full often hath she gossiped by my side and sat with me on Neptune's yellow sands.'

'If I may tear you away, Roy, interrupted Nurse Nielsen from the corridor. Oxygen is low. We need an F and two ZDs.' She continued her round. Roy touched the window blind.

'Open or closed?'

'Open.'

'I bet you were magic.'

Frances blew Roy a kiss, as he gently closed the side room door.

Norton sat in his sinking chair, polishing off a large helping of curry. Roy stepped onto the roof.

'Hi, the boiler parts have arrived.'

Norton laid a huge towel on the warm asphalt.

'Hit the deck for a minute. Keep me company.'

Roy lay back and closed his eyes. 'Do you ever think about death? You know, your own death?'

'No. Good food. Wednesday's always best.'

'Where's your van?'

'It's parked on the caravan site next door.'

'Oh, OK.'

'Do you like driving?'

'I guess.'

'Have you thought about driving a real ambulance? Racing through town on a blue light must be good ... with the siren blaring. Of course you'd need some training.'

'I'm getting training right now, from my line manager, Agnieszka.'

'What does she know?'

'She's got a degree in elect ... electromechanical engineering. Warsaw University.'

'Fancy that.'

Norton scraped the remaining rice into the carpark below. Two gulls fought over the morsels. Roy watched attentively, as Norton installed the new circuit board and replaced two temperature sensors. He restored the power and watched the panel as it scrolled through various self-tests. 'Initialization Complete' remained on the display.

'Time for a celebratory roll-up, mate.'

They returned to their positions on the roof. Norton deftly assembled a cigarette and lit it. He inhaled deeply.

'What do you want to do when you get away from here?'

'I haven't thought about getting away. Something in the funeral business, maybe, eventually.'

'Too tall, aren't you? To be a bearer? The coffin would be at an angle.'

'Professional wrestler?'

'Now you're talking.'

Norton raised his tee-shirt to display a dragon tattoo across most of his back. 'You'll need to get a few of these. Marco did this. He's an artist. Don't go to any old high-street cowboy.'

'I won't.'

Roy pretended to admire the oddly deformed design. He wouldn't have known it was a dragon, had he not been told. Norton held out his strangely sweet-smelling cigarette.

'Not even a puff?'

'I don't smoke.'

'Right answer. Fighters have to watch their health.'

Roy's second facilities training session was the maintenance of door furniture; a few of the hospice door locks got stuck when the temperature was too high or too low. Agnieszka adjusted a large magnifying light and unscrewed a mortice lock. She carefully removed each of the levers and placed them on tissue paper.

'Never oil a mortice lock. They work by gravity and these levers must be free to slide against each other. See?' With a pinch of talcum powder, she massaged each lever and returned them to the spindle in sequence. She replaced the plate and moved the deadlock back and forth. 'Simple physics. You should clean all of them once a year.'

It was almost going home time. Passing the laundry, Roy was waylaid by the two Marias, who were determined to take his photograph with their phones.

'She like the sound of you Roy, boy. I tell her you beautiful. Wants to see for herself.'

'Is this your niece again?'

'Yes yes. Hold still.'

'Has she got a name?'

'He interested!' Both women laughed. One of them gently pushed Roy backwards and made a note of his height on the wall with a marker pen.

'She wants to know if you tall. Very tall, I say.' 'Big and strong,' added the other Maria. Roy made for the door. 'She won't wait long ...'

Two more patients had joined Wednesday transport. The thin man with discoloured hands sat on his own. It was his turn to be dropped off last. As the minibus turned on to Tennyson Avenue, the man moved a few seats forward.

'Can we stop here for a minute or two?'

Roy pulled over and switched off the engine; he was used to this patient request. They both watched a sprinkler showering each side of a manicured lawn in turn, like a metronome.

'Can you keep a secret?'

'I keep lots of secrets,' answered Roy. He was always uncertain about such moments. How could he promise to keep a secret if he didn't know what it was. He reasoned that many secrets only need to be kept until the patient's death.

'I was unfaithful to my wife ... for six years.'

Roy had heard this one before. 'I said nothing. It's too late to tell her now.'

They sat silently for a couple of minutes. Afternoon light refracted through the garden spray.

'Well, what do you think?' asked the man.

'How long were you married?'

'Eighteen years.'

'And was your wife happy?'

'She often told me she was.'

'I think she must have really loved you.'

'She didn't know I spent time with another woman.'

'Six years? She knew.'

Roy recalled the apposite observation from one of his Reader's Digest books; it was the perfect balm.

'You're a wise head on young shoulders, you know that? Thank you, driver.'

Roy didn't feel wise sitting in his literacy class. He was the only learner without a letter, although one was now writing itself in his head, 'Dear Roy - No wonder you were abandoned. You're just a useless ...'

'Roy?'

Roy looked up at his tutor. There was a new project on the board and the other learners were working in pairs. The tutor sat beside him.

'May I see?'

She slowly pulled his worksheet from beneath Roy's dagger-like pen. His scribbling had almost torn through the page. This is exactly how he used to feel at school. If he could just run from the building and hide in Madame Kezia's kiosk on the seafront; The fortune teller would tell him once again that everything was going to be all right.

'It's the pen. It's not working.'

The tutor replaced the pen and paper. 'I think you'll enjoy this week's activity. We're going to each write a description of the town we live in.'

'Writing to describe. Adjectives.'

'Exactly. In a few minutes, we're going to brainstorm a selection of words we might use.'

'Sunny. Windy.'

'Good words. I'll come to you first.'

The tutor wiped the board clean. Roy's phone vibrated in his pocket – the sixth call of the evening. He furtively checked the incoming list: private number ... no message. He settled the pen in his left hand and carefully formed the letters of a new adjective – dangerous.

'Where's my bike! Goddammit,' Roy shouted at the empty bike rack. He glowered at his useless lock, broken and twisted on the ground. He wandered away from the library, then turned back. He picked up the lock and threw it into a bin.

CHAPTER NINE

Autumn

***

Friday felt like a day of change. Dried leaves held noisy chariot races in the carpark and the shadows were noticeably longer; summer was coming to an end. While Roy was bagging the leaves, he discovered the cat was dead. 'Just double bag it and bin it,' Agnieszka suggested. Rather unceremonious, he thought, but what alternative was there? He delivered his weekly laundry to the Marias. They checked his bedsheet with forensic interest, in search, it seemed, for evidence of his fecundity. It was merely a couple of small tears that would be darned before the end of the day. After the fire alarm test and a fighter-size portion of fish and chips, Roy vigorously battled his way through the daily tasks.

Like a bank teller, Mrs King counted out a number of bank notes on her desk. She placed the money in an envelope and handed it to Roy.

'You see, if you had bought that fridge, you wouldn't have had enough to replace your bike. Sometimes things work out for the best.'

Roy knew he would have to budget carefully to get through the next two weeks. The cash would be enough for a reasonable second-hand machine, but he'd have to ask Bernice for some weekend food. He checked his phone for the fifth time that day. He was relieved to see no more private calls had come in. With some time spare, he sought solace with Norton, who was sunbathing on the roof.

'Maybe it was something it ate,' Norton suggested sheepishly. It's feral isn't it.'

'I suppose it was.'

'Could be the rat poison you put down.'

'I wonder if animals feel sad when one of them dies.'

'They do. Some birds hold funerals. Crows.'

'Seriously? Do you know about birds?'

'Not much. It was a pub quiz question. A crow flies down and tries mating the dead bird back to life. Has sex with it.'

Roy continued to look nonplussed.

'You OK, mate? You've not heard about that?' Roy shook his head doubtfully. 'Elephants, too ... they have funerals. I don't think any sex is involved. Have you ever seen an elephant?'

'On TV. Have you?'

'No. It's on my bucket list.'

With every patient safely ferried home, Roy hosed down the minibus and practised his backing vocals. It was the end of the week and everything was going to be all right. He had one hundred pounds in his pocket. Tomorrow, he would buy some new wheels.

Roy woke to a sun-filled room. He could barely remember arriving home and collapsing on the unmade bed. Unfolding his laundry, he discovered another decorated bookmark from the Marias. As well as the sheets, a torn seam in his underpants had been lovingly repaired with red cotton thread. After showering, he laid his charity shop suit on the neatly-made bed. This Saturday was going to be different.

Once the floral tributes were delivered, Roy attached his clip-on tie and confidently entered the crematorium. Michael Pappas' service began at noon, but relatives and friends had been milling around for an hour or more. The mourners looked unusually relaxed, as if they attended services every day. Everyone became still and quiet, when a stretched limousine pulled up at the main door. Mrs Pappas entered the building, with a huge nephew on either side. Once she was seated on the front row, a queue formed to give condolences. The small woman looked implacable, as everyone bowed and mumbled. The word Theós could be heard repeatedly. Roy followed suit.

'Theós?'

The woman looked up and grasped Roy's hand. For a moment, family attendees looked uncomfortable, as if this was a gesture of succession. Roy sat on his own as six pallbearers carried Michael's coffin to the catafalque. After minutes of coughing and throat clearing, a Greek lamentation blared from the PA system. Roy's mind wandered. He asked himself a question about cremated teeth; did pieces of enamel survive the fire? Would they be left in the ashes? He would have to ask Reddington Funeral Directors; they'd know what ended up in the urn. The coffin finally rolled slowly to the other side and a sliding curtain ended the proceedings. Strolling back to the delivery van, Roy half expected to see the elfin woman lurking in the car park. The neat row of expensive cars offered rich pickings.

Reversing the delivery van into its parking bay, Roy observed two uniformed police officers speaking to Gina inside her shop. Sitting at his bedsit window, he was able to hear their conversation. A 'young person' had been murdered during the night. Gina had already sold three bouquets for the victim. The police wanted the customers' descriptions and details of the credit card transactions. Apparently, it was not unusual for the perpetrator or their accomplices to purchase a floral tribute.

Despite the approaching storm, Roy walked to the town centre. Finding the bike shop closed, he continued to the scene of the crime: a narrow, windowless side street through which shoplifters often made their escape. A number of posies marked the spot, surrounded by glowing tea lights. A blurry enlargement of a small portrait was attached to a drainpipe – a smiling boy who would never be fifteen. A few teenagers stared at the impromptu memorial. An older woman was reading the various dedications - 'Probably a plainclothes cop,' thought Roy.

He sloped off and walked despondently along the promenade. A peal of thunder made him feel disquieted. As if on cue, his phone rang: private caller. No message. When the rain arrived, he hurriedly retraced his steps through the side streets, heading for home. A single figure now stood at the memorial, their face hidden by the hood of a long plastic mac. Sheltering in a shop doorway, Roy watched the statue-still figure for minutes. When the figure turned and continued down the side street, he knew who it was: the elfin woman. Roy ran after her. Realising she was being chased, the woman darted around some bins and hid between two skips. When Roy pulled alongside, she pulled a knife from her pocket.

'I'll use it.'

Roy stood still. He could see she was afraid. 'I doubt it.'

Tucked into a corner booth at the Seashell Café, Roy studied the woman, who leant against a padded plastic bolster, her eyes barely open.

'You're tired.'

'Tired and hungry,' she quietly replied.

He pushed the menu across the table. The woman looked older than before. Her hands were thin and scarred. Her fingernails were bitten to the quick, with traces of nail polish. In close-up, not elfin, but scrawny.

'Can you pay for this, or are we doing a runner?'

'This is on me. The kid who was stabbed. Did you know him?'

'Why have you been following me?'

'I haven't.'

'Well, I know your face.'

'I saw you in the registry office. You were getting married.'

'Ah, yes. Hilarious.'

'Are you frightened of your husband?'

'One more question and I'm gone.'

After some food, the woman became more relaxed and spoke candidly about her exploits. Stealing from cars had just become a habit. The real money came from hospital raids, 'Find a sleeping patient and take their handbag ... housekeys and address in one go'. The young woman admitted to 'doing the hospice' a couple of times, 'cash, keys and morphine ... what's not to like?' She spoke brazenly about her housebreaking skills.

'Don't look so shocked. I never hurt anyone.'

'Someone always gets hurt. What about your knife?'

'Protection. I've never used it.'

She wiped her soup spoon on a napkin and held it up for Roy to see his shocked reflection.

'The look on your face. Like you've never done anything wrong?'

'The man in the registration office ...'

'Some Albanian, wanting to stay in the country. I was promised five grand for that. I haven't seen a penny. Never will see a penny. They're bloody criminals.'

'Who are *they?'*

'Don't pretend you don't know. They've got a picture of you ... driving your hospice van.'

'Beano? Slightly crazy, with bleached hair?'

'Bingo. Beano and Napoleon. They think they're gangsters. They're just a pair of art school wankers. Five grand. I could be living in Florida.'
She leaned across the table, her hands held in supplication. 'Will you help me? I need to get away.'

'Where?'

'Anywhere. I can't go back to my flat. I'm going to get on a bus today ... or a train.'

A waitress placed their bill on the table.

'Pay at the till.'

'I don't normally have to pay. My money is no good here,' mumbled Roy. He looked up, but the waitress had already left.

'Please, pleaded the woman quietly.'

Roy took the brown wage packet from his zip pocket. He unfolded a few notes. 'How much is the train?'

'I need to go a long way.' In one swift and easy movement, she took all of the money. She left one note beside the bill and stuffed the rest into her jeans.

I'll get it back to you, I promise.'

The woman sped away, leaving nothing but a trace of cheap scent. It took a few moments for Roy to realise what had just happened; he'd been mugged.

He looked inside the envelope, to check that it was empty. The elderly café owner placed a cappuccino on the table and smiled ruefully.

'On the house, Roy.'

'How could he have been so stupid? Roy leant against his pillows, listening to the rain. With two pounds to his name, it wasn't worth making his weekly supermarket visit. He'd get to work early in the morning and stoke up in the refectory. And, since he was walking to The Beeches, he'd need to leave forty minutes earlier. He could say he'd lost the money – not untrue. Mrs King was sure to advance enough for his bus fares. He took his scissors to the last intact copy of Reader's Digest. After reading about a widow who gave one of her kidneys to a stranger, he felt happier; maybe his recent loss was of little consequence. He put the story into his shoebox.

CHAPTER TEN

Although Monday was unusually cold, walking to work was a piece of cake. Roy didn't know why he hadn't tried it before. He enjoyed the chirps and trills of birds in hawthorn hedges as they feasted on berries. His joy evaporated when he picked up a Confirmatory Medical Certificate, that had been pushed under the facilities room door: Frances Antonia Dyer, 61 years, stage 4 metastatic melanoma with liver metastases, 04:25, exhaustion. So many patients died in the small hours, he observed idly. He didn't want to see Frances' body. He wanted to keep her alive in his mind for the next day or two. She'd been one of his first passengers. Her easy laughter and the smell of bourbon on her breath would linger awhile.

Bernice placed a mountainous fry-up on Roy's table. 'I don't want you losing weight. Speaking of weight, your fat hot water friend was in last week, helping himself to anything and everything. He should know we're not a charity. Well, we are, but not for him.'

'He was just in to check the boiler,' Roy said reassuringly. 'I don't expect you'll see him again.'

'Good, or Mrs King gets to see him off.'

Despite his own hunger, Roy covered his mountainous breakfast and took it up to the roof space. Norton was lounging on the roof, transferring the weekend's lottery numbers to his pink notebook.

'Got one of the lottery numbers. Most I've ever had is three. Money in the bank.' He closed the book with a theatrical snapping action. 'That for me? Cheers, mate.'

Norton took a fork from his pocket, wiped it on his overalls and fell upon the plate of food. Roy explained that it was 'best to lie low'.

'Lie low on the roof?' Norton enjoyed his own joke. 'I'll be leaving soon. I've got another job coming up ... down the coast.'

'That's good ... having another job.'

'It's a convent. They're bound to have room under their rafters.'

'Haven't you got a home?' Asked Roy, gingerly.

'Not anymore. Wife chucked me out. Fair enough.' Roy waited for more details, but none came. Norton returned the plate. 'What's the pudding today?'

'Monday? It's usually something with custard.'

'Lovely. Only if you have time.'

The undertakers arrived for Frances. Roy looked away as they transferred her body. He pocketed the three coins; it's what she would have wanted, he reasoned. He was immediately summoned to Mrs King's office, where he received some good news: his bicycle had been found. He could collect it today, after his passenger run.

Roy knew the town police station well. He began his life there, abandoned, in a supermarket bag-for-life, between two silver birch trees on the driveway. He'd often imagined his mother setting him down and hurrying back along the approach road. Was she tall and good-looking? Young or old? The only thing he knew was that she'd made a mistake. The smell of disinfectant in the station entrance made him feel strangely at home; such institutions were pretty much the same, with the constant echo of slamming doors. Collecting his bike wasn't going to be as simple as he'd hoped. The desk sergeant led him to a windowless interview room where he waited. What had sounded like good news initially now curdled in his mind. A detective entered and sat with a loud sigh.

'I'm getting too old for this.' The detective did look too old for this – a crumpled man who couldn't afford to retire. His friendly smile put Roy at ease, momentarily. The Detective opened a police file and flicked through a few pages. He closed the file and tapped it respectfully. 'Roy Birch. That's quite a story. How are you these days?'

'I'm good. My bike was stolen. I locked it outside the library.'

'How do we know the bicycle we recovered belongs to you, Roy?'

'The postcode? I scratched it under the crossbar.'

'Tell me about Friday night.'

The bike had been recovered from Half Moon Lane at midnight. Of course, he knew where the lane was; he'd lived in the town all his life. The Detective used the word coincidence more than once and showed him the grainy reproduction of a teenager's school photograph. Roy stated clearly that he'd heard about the murder from his landlady. He'd visited the makeshift memorial on Saturday afternoon.

'Why?' wondered the policeman

Roy shrugged and looked at the CCTV camera high on the wall. 'There were quite a few people there.'

'But why were *you* there?'

'I wanted to know what had happened.'

'But you already knew what had happened.'

Roy crossed his arms. He wasn't interested in playing this old ping pong game. 'I'm parked right outside. Will I be fined?'

'You should be fine.'

The Detective asked a few more questions, but he too had decided that he'd prefer to be somewhere else. He stood up with a groan and eased his aching back.

'My sergeant will meet you at the back door. Just ring the bell.'

Lifting his bike into the minibus, Roy noticed that the handlebar and grips had been cleaned. He realised that it would have been checked for fingerprints and DNA. Since they already had both of his, he guessed he was in the clear.

Feeling that he'd been let off once today, Roy dropped the undertakers' three coins into the facilities room jar. He knew that pocketing the gratuity once could so easily become a habit. The sound made Agnieszka look up from her local newspaper.

'Who's that?'

'Frances Dyer. Side Room Three. I'm going to her funeral on Saturday. It's a burial. I've never been to one.'

'Make sure you take an umbrella. That's a golden rule. Did you bring her stuff down?'

Roy swivelled and reached into a plastic crate. He placed the deceased's effects onto his desk: collected poems volume one, collected poems volume two, hairbrush, empty make-up bag and a hip flask. Agnieszka removed the cap and sniffed.

'Pewter. Nice.' She placed it in her desk drawer, for safekeeping. 'I'll look after that. Someone may come looking for it. Did she have any relatives visit?'

'I don't think so. She told me she had a sister.'

Agnieszka returned to the local newspaper. 'You heard about the boy who was killed? There's nothing about it in the paper. It must have missed the deadline.'

Roy placed the two books into his backpack, for safekeeping.

When Roy pulled up outside the familiar house on Rose Gardens, his Monday regulars wondered what they were doing here. This was the first time he'd driven to the house of a deceased patient. He apologised and quickly closed the passenger door. He was intrigued to see a young man taking photographs of Frances' property. Dressed in a powder blue suit and yellow tie, the man was clearly not a funeral director. Roy ferried his silent passengers to their homes and headed back to The Beeches. Cycling home seemed such a sweet way to end the day. There'd been no damage to the machine. Someone had even adjusted the gears, so that they now changed more smoothly. He carried his prize possession into the bedsit and flopped onto his bed. When the bedhead hit the wall noisily, he realised that the whole bedframe had been moved a few centimetres. Walking around the room, he saw that other objects were not in their usual position. A book had been left open face down. That was something he'd never do, having being told by one of the Marias that it brought bad luck; he'd clearly had a visitor.

'Everything all right? I heard a banging noise.'

Roy opened his window to see Gina in the yard. 'Someone's been in my room.'

'Me, my love. A couple of policewomen wanted a quick look.'

'No one asked me.'

'They didn't have to. You're the lodger and I'm the landlady.'

'What were they looking for?'

'I really couldn't say. I was going to ask you the same question. They didn't take anything.' Roy started a question twice, but stalled. Gina fidgeted with a pair of secateurs. 'Anyway, I must get on. I'm working on two wreaths for a ten-forty cremation.'

CHAPTER ELEVEN

On Tuesday, the hospice entrance resembled an A&E department, with three ambulances parked outside. Three admissions meant three beds. Nurse Nielsen looked like a flight controller, as her staff shuffled furniture around the main ward. The side rooms were soon full, except for Six, because the cleaning staff feared the haunted room. Roy was required to spend an hour alone, scrubbing, mopping, wiping and dusting. As he moved his yellow bucket energetically back and forth, he was watched by one of the newly-arrived patients, who occupied a handsome wing chair. When Roy emerged, the man applauded loudly - surprisingly loudly, given his physical condition.

'Well done. I can imagine you wowing the hoi polloi in the Coliseum.' Roy didn't know what the elderly man had just said, but thought it was probably complimentary. 'Charles Devereux. Do you remember me?'

It took a moment for Roy to recall the man he collected from Lapwing Cottage weeks before; the man who alarmed his fellow passengers and fled the day centre at the first opportunity. Without his hat, the man looked much older, with thinning hair and pronounced veins on his temples. The man leaned heavily on a walking frame, as Roy skilfully manoeuvred the wing chair through the narrow door in one, effortless movement. Patients were allowed to bring a few possessions for their stay. This was the largest anyone had seen.

'There, the nurses said it wouldn't go in ... fifteen love, I think.' Devereux followed Roy into Side Room Six and took a deep breath. 'Industrial lemon scent, with a hint of lime. I've smelt worse.'

'Where would you like it, Mr Devereux?'

'Facing the window. I can watch the birds and lonely clouds.' Devereux collapsed into his favourite chair. 'A room with a view.' He watched patiently as Roy demonstrated the articulated bed switchgear and showed the function of each wall switch.

'Anything you need ... press this red button.'

'Je suis contente. Pourboire. Devereux held out a banknote.'

'Thank you, but staff are not allowed to accept gifts.'

'Sterling sentiments. Man to man, Roy.' Devereux stared at Roy and kept his arm outstretched. Roy took the money and opened the door. 'Please leave it open. I need to hear the hubbub.'

Carrying the cleaning gear back through the ward, Roy's path was blocked by Nurse Nielsen, who held out an empty hospice collection box. He folded the banknote and dutifully pushed it slowly through the slot.

Roy wrapped two slices of pizza and spent lunchtime on the roof. Norton's sleeping bag and food canisters suggested that the heating engineer was still in residence. Roy relaxed in the chair and flicked through the pink lottery book by its side. He saw that many of the pages had been recently defaced with wild biro swirls. Other pages had been torn from the damaged book and strewn across the roof. Roy carefully collected the lost pages and placed everything beside Norton's other possessions.

Devereux's presence continued to disconcert the staff and patients throughout the day. Reading an amusing novel, he produced loud guffaws and comments addressed to no-one in particular. When Nurse Nielsen tried to pull his door to, Devereux assumed a faux accusatory tone and threatened to sue the next person who attempted to lock him in. The Chaplain also got short shrift. Nurses took any route they could to avoid passing Devereux's room.

'Close the door, Roy.' He sat and waited while Mrs King collated papers and prevented a pile of paper files from leaning any further. 'It's a very busy time. We lost another of our nursing staff this afternoon. She had to return to Portugal.'

'I'm sorry to hear that.'

'Yes.' The manager stared at the wall behind Roy, then re-straightened her files. 'It's a wonder we manage. You've met Mr. Devereux, of course. Agnieszka has asked that you deal with any of his maintenance requests. I'm sure he won't make too much trouble.' Roy wondered how much trouble a dying man could make. 'If you notice anything untoward, then please report that directly to me.'

'What's untoward?'

'Speaking inappropriately to the staff.'

'Ah, OK.'

'Splendid news about your bicycle.' The Manager squeezed out a sad smile.

Returning to his bedsit, Roy discovered four unanswered calls on his work phone. He lay on his bed, staring at the receiver, as yet another call invaded his privacy: private number, private number, private number. Perhaps it was just spam, or someone calling to sell him something? Was he worrying too much? ... but who calls to sell you something at eight o'clock? No, this was something bad; he felt it in his bones. He decided that he would answer the next call; he should at least listen. Two hours later, the phone rang again.

'Yes?'

'Hello, Roy.' The quiet voice sounded thin and distant. 'Whatever you feel like doing, do not hang up. Do you understand? Roy?'

'OK'

'You know who this is?'

'Napoleon.'

'Have you thought about our offer? Are you still there?'

'Sure.'

'You're sure? About what?'

'I'm still here.'

'It's just that we have a new vacancy. After hours.'

The caller's words swam in Roy's ear, becoming less distinct. A minute later, he merely heard his name being repeated: Roy? Roy? He closed his phone and lay still in the dark, silent room. The tapping blind woke him before dawn. He'd left his window wide open and an autumn wind was getting up to speed. With time to kill, Roy cycled to work along the promenade. Disassembled fairground rides were being loaded onto trailers for the journey to winter pasture. On the glistening pebble beach, two familiar hospice visitors held up an urn, trying to gift their relative's ashes to the sea. The strong wind sent a spiral of ash around the alarmed mourners. Arriving early at the hospice, Roy had time to complete his writing task for the evening class. On his last visit to the library, he had helped himself to a handful of tourist leaflets. He proceeded to copy raw chunks of text, that extolled the virtues of his town: not one he recognised. The tutor would commend him for his progress, but she'd clearly lost interest in this student. She had her favourites and Roy would never be one. He was pleased to be interrupted by his first call of the day – maintenance to Side Room Six.

Devereux was slumped against one side of his wing chair, a pillow about to fall. Roy lifted thc man with ease and seated him comfortably. He rescued a book that had fallen to the floor.

'A friendly face, at last.' Devereux rubbed his arm vigorously. 'Losing all feeling.'

'Shall I fetch a nurse?'

'No. Not Nielsen with her moue ... or the evangelical Christian singing hymns as she doles out the painkillers.'

'That's Precious Adaugo. She's from Nigeria.'

'That's the one.'

'She's really nice. The staff work very long hours.'

'Of course they do,' replied Devereux apologetically. 'How rude of me. Bloody awful night. It's these things they give you to suck.'

'Oramorph.'

'Gives one the weirdest dreams.'

'I've never tried one.'

Devereux chuckled and clenched his fists. 'I'm losing all sensation.'

'They told me your light wasn't working.'

Devereux gestured to the wall-mounted Anglepoise. 'It keeps flickering. It's difficult to read.'

Roy removed the screw-in bulb and blew onto the electrical contacts. He replaced the bulb which lit-up Devereux's appreciative face.

'You make it look easy. Good, I can return to The Aegean. Have you read The Odyssey?'

Roy shook his head slowly. 'It looks like an old book.'

Devereux ran his fingers along the discoloured Sellotape binding repair. 'An old book, certainly ... and much loved. Are you the only man in this establishment, Roy?'

'Most of the time. We have a heating engineer. He sometimes visits.'

'And your harem serves you well?' Roy looked confused. 'Your colleagues are kind to you?'

'Always.' Devereux stared at Roy. 'Can I fix any ...' continued Roy.

'My apologies. I was just thinking of something long ago.'

Roy stepped into the corridor and pulled the door to. 'Leave it open?'

'Always. Hubbub.'

As Roy walked through the ward, a middle-age patient removed her headphones and beckoned him.

'Who is the man who's been making all the noise?'

'I don't know about any noise.'

'Laughing his head off in the small hours ... and won't let anyone close his door. Hey, Roy, did you hear Mrs Warren went in the night?' The woman pointed a fat finger at the unoccupied bed opposite. She couldn't resist a mischievous smile. 'Madam Warren was such a stuck-up cow. She thought she could outlast me.'

'I knew you could do it,' Roy said playfully. 'See you around.'

There was no sign of Norton having returned. The pink notebook was where Roy had placed it, next to the sleeping bag and food packets. He left a phone message for the engineer, to remind. Reddington Funeral Directors arrived for Mrs Warren. Only one of the usual undertakers stood in the corridor, like a single bookend, his eyes closed and head bowed. As Roy unlocked the mortuary door, the sad-looking man explained that his work partner of seven years had died the previous day.

'It was a heart attack. And I heard his last words, 'I'm not feeling very well', he said ... then he collapsed. The undertaker snapped his fingers. Any one of us ... at any time. Strange to think I'll soon be bearing him on my shoulder. Will you give me a hand?' Roy held Mrs Warren's legs and transferred her to the temporary coffin. 'We'll be looking for someone to join us at Reddington, if you're interested.'

'I'm all right, thanks, at the moment,' replied Roy, disagreeably reminded of the last employment offer. Thoughts of mortality stayed with him through his overcooked lasagne lunch. Even Bernice with her flirting and wrestling anecdotes failed to raise his spirits. With no lock for his bike, he walked to the literacy class. A library notice informed him that this evening's session had been cancelled due to ill health. As he was close to the town centre, he felt compelled to visit Half Moon Lane. The makeshift memorial was now practically gone: a single, decomposing bouquet beneath the boy's frozen portrait. Noticing a police car parked at the far end of the lane, Roy pulled up his collar and left. As he walked along the thoroughfare, a municipal surveillance camera tracked his movements.

As one of The Marias inspected Roy's Friday load of laundry, her inseparable companion scrolled through recently received images of her unmarried niece. Their usual sales talk was replaced with comically serious looks of disappointment.

'No-one getting younger,' they chanted in unison.

Roy slumped into his swivel chair and checked his tray for any new death certificates. Agnieszka looked up from her local newspaper.

'Has Ann Warren been collected?'

'Yesterday. One of the Reddington undertakers died this week.'

'I heard about that ... and look at this.' Agnieszka licked her fingers and turned the pages back with a flourish. Roy scanned the newspaper. Between two clothing sales announcements, was the report of a fatal traffic accident. A photograph showed a red transit van on its side, the cab burnt-out. The mugshot below identified the victim as James Norton.

'He was our heating man, wasn't he?'

Roy ran his finger along the printed text. 'Van left the road ... Tuesday ten o'clock ... driver four times over the alcohol limit. I didn't know he drank. No other vehicle involved. Unbelievable. He was a nice man.'

'He was out of his head, insisted Agnieszka.'

Roy trudged up to the roof and stuffed Norton's remaining possession into a couple of bin liners. It had been a while since he sang any radio hits, or even listened to the radio; it was clearly a day to think about the fragility of life. He returned to the facilities room with Norton's pink notebook, its pages held together with an elastic band.

'Agnieszka, do you ever play the National Lottery?'

'Most weeks. You?'

'Never. It's a mug's game ... apparently.'

'Thanks.'

'How would I check last Saturday's numbers?'

Roy turned to the front page of the notebook, while Agnieszka found the Lottery website. As she read out the winning numbers, Roy ran his finger along Norton's originally selected numbers; they corresponded exactly. Norton's number had come up.

'Two winners, sharing nine million pounds. Ticket holders from Liverpool and Sunderland. Maybe I should move,' mused Agnieszka.

Roy dropped the damaged notebook into his waste bin. A call from the ward brought him abruptly back to Earth: reading light out in Side Room Six.

Devereux looked as puzzled as Roy, to see the Anglepoise bulb was missing.

'Someone must have come into my room during the night.'

'Why would? ...' Roy looked around the skirting and under the bed.

'Probably taken by another patient. I'm not universally liked.'

'Such a weird thing to do.' Roy took a bulb from the neighbouring room and fixed the problem.

'Parfait.'

'Sorry?'

'I'm just making light.'

'OK, well, if your light plays ...'

'Please.' Devereux gestured to the visitor chair.

Roy sat with a sigh. 'You're tired.' It wasn't a question, so it went unanswered. Roy didn't know whether he should leave or not. The weight he felt on his shoulders pressed him down onto the chair.

'It's just ... been a very weird week.'

'How so?'

'People dying.'

'Isn't it an occupational hazard?'

'Friends. Not friends exactly, but people I know ... outside the hospice.'

'They come not single spies but in battalions.'

Roy's train of thought was skewed by the old man's abstruse response.

'It's time to collect the patients.' Roy left the side room door open and slowly descended the emergency stairs. He snapped his fingers. The crisp sound that echoed through the stairwell was not as pleasing as it should have been. The Friday passengers were all new to Roy; his regulars had departed. A new patient on Keats Avenue had dyed her hair crimson red.

'What the hell,' she said, 'My last hurrah.'

CHAPTER TWELVE

Saturday was overcast and unusually cold. It seemed appropriate for Frances' funeral. Roy laid his suit on the bed and unfolded his freshly laundered shirt. Discovering a small packet of Filipino apple candy in the breast pocket, he smiled. With four services scheduled, Gina loaded a stack of wreathes into the delivery van and gave Roy six yellow roses for his friend's grave. Behind the crematorium, he neatly set out the floral tributes in order, took an umbrella from the delivery van and made his way to the far end of the cemetery. A couple of fresh graves had appeared since his last visit, with clods of earth partially concealing temporary plaques. Today's grave was almost two metres deep, with an apron of artificial grass to prevent the bearers from slipping on the mud. With no-one else in sight, Roy wondered whether he'd got the time wrong. When it started to rain, he opened the umbrella. He was slightly disconcerted to find 'Gina's Flowers' printed in bright letters, along with the flower shop's phone number. A hearse and a long limousine approached. Two mourners and the celebrant stepped out of the seven-seater and nodded to Roy. He recognised the man he'd last seen in Frances' Garden, still wearing a powder blue suit. The women pulled up the hood of her orange, plastic raincoat. Roy thought that Frances would have appreciated these splashes of colour. The celebrant pulled up her hood and stamped her feet to stay warm.

The hand-painted coffin was positioned on timber supports. The eulogy painted a picture of a wonderful life: many parts played and many battles won. Frances' notes did cover a few pages. The celebrant lost her place a couple of times and skipped a paragraph or two. Roy carefully positioned his six roses on the coffin and watched the burial.
When the man in powder blue approached, Roy shared his umbrella.

'Thank you. Gordon P. Clark - National Association of Estate Agents. I'm Frances' nephew. Lovely woman. Sad.'

'Roy Birch.'

'Of course. You drive the hospice bus.'

'Driver, porter and facilities assistant.'

'Of course, yes. My aunt thought highly of you. It seems you're in the know.'

'About what?'

'Which properties might be coming up for sale ... probate sales. Relatives usually want to expedite these things. It's my agency's speciality. We offer a generous finder's fee.'

'Who's the finder?'

'That would be you. With patient details, we can give the executor a realistic valuation and sales plan. You would receive a quarter of one percent.'

The estate agent placed a few business cards into Roy's breast pocket. 'My private number is on there, OK?'

'Who was the woman in orange?'

'An old friend. I can't remember her name. They were both in a medical TV drama for years.'

'I don't watch television.'

'Who does. Anyway, I think it's about to pour down.'

Roy sat in the delivery van, his vision obscured by the downpour. He thought about the ceremony and hoped that more people would attend his own funeral: how easy it was to be forgotten.

Roy spent Sunday indoors, occasionally looking out at the continuing flow of water in the road. He tuned his radio to Sounds of The Eighties, a music quiz and the local weather forecast. He was hungry and flat broke, so a wet dash to the supermarket wasn't an option. He slept until the small hours, when the sound of a barking dog blended with his unhappy dreams. The rain receded and he lay still, listening to the dawn chorus. Switching on his phone, he discovered two more missed calls: private number.

The hospice was silent, too exhausted to feign any signs of life. Roy entered the door code and dragged a drenched stack of weekend donations into reception. He recovered a two-legged chair that had been abandoned in the corridor and a greetings card, taped to the facilities office door.

To all nursing staff and allied health professionals and building maintenance staff. In the cycle of thanksgiving – you were remembered today at the service of reflection in the prayer room, and thanks were given for the work that you do in the hospice: Chaplain.

Bernice wouldn't be raising the shutter on her breakfast counter for another hour. He put his feet up and enjoyed some well-earned sleep.

The first call of the day was 'light out in Side Room Six'. Roy grabbed a pack of new bulbs.

'Does the whole lamp need replacing?' wondered Devereux.

Roy cleaned the light contacts again and replaced the bulb.

'It's just the bulb. Maybe we've bought a faulty batch. They're meant to last for ages. Two thousand hours, according to the box ... that's months.'

'It should outlast me, certainly. Good weekend?'

Roy shrugged in response. 'It was all go here. Our Nigerian friend ...'

'Precious Adaugo.'

'Precious played The Messiah to the whole ward. It doesn't sound appealing, but I rather enjoyed it. Shall we talk?' Devereux gestured to the visitor's chair.

'I'd like to, but it's quite a busy morning.'

'Of course. When you have time.'

Roy had time. He just didn't have the will or energy to chat with a man who had so little time. Surely Devereux would be happier finding out what happens in his old book. Roy set about cleaning the bins – his least favourite monthly task. The high-pressure water spray tore into aged bags of rubbish stuck to the sides, creating a small, fetid lake. The smell made him gag. He cautiously rescued some syringe needles, that never made it into a sharps box. His wonderful new life was beginning to pall. After the summer months, the town now looked drab; even his bedsit felt smaller. Filling the hospice minibus with fuel, he turned to the faded petrol station billboard, that he read on every visit to the petrol station: PREGNANT MOTHER IN CHRISTMAS TREE BLAZE. The stale, enigmatic announcement begged a hundred questions. There was more cleaning up to be done in the afternoon, when the hospice's giant yucca plant gave up the ghost. It fell on the reception desk and spilled soil across the floor. Manoeuvring his blue cleaning bucket, Roy thought about the undertaker's suggestion. Perhaps it was time to change jobs. He could drive and he owned a suit, but was he too tall to be a pall-bearer? The day ended with his favourite task: washing out the minibus. Blasting the vehicle with a spray produced a pleasing rainbow effect against the evening sun. Looking back to the building, his eye was drawn to Side Room Six. Devereux was silhouetted against the interior lights. Roy returned the man's wave. He'd forgotten to check on the patient; he'd visit first thing in the morning.

As Roy carried his bike up the bedsit stairs, his phone rang for the third time. He let it ring twice again before answering.

'Roy?' The elfin woman's whispered voice filled his ear.

'Who is this?'

'You know who it is. I need you to listen.' The woman said she had to see him this evening. She wanted to return the money she borrowed before leaving town.

'You're very quiet,' replied Roy.

'I can't raise my voice.'

Roy remained silent as the woman gave instructions. She ended mid-sentence; the call cut off. What was he to think? How had the woman got his number? Was she in trouble? He wrote down the few details he could recall and pulled on his jacket.

An ancient man peered over his door chain and threatened to call the police. A young family filled their front doorway and offered a dozen different suggestions: had he got the number wrong? Had he misheard? Did he know there were four streets with a similar name? The street lights kicked in to life as Roy rode his bike through the town. A police car drew level momentarily. Roy dismounted and entered a side alley; he didn't want to get stopped for not having lights. Back in his bedsit, he waited for the next call, but it never came.

It was an unsettled night on the wards. Three deaths, tearful relatives and a skeleton nursing staff ensured that no-one slept. Devereux closed his side room door and read for five hours straight, trying to ignore the commotion. When his eyes eventually closed and the book fell to the floor, Sister Nielsen marched down the corridor, conducting her daily reveille. Devereux removed the bulb from his Anglepoise and reached behind his chair cushion for the original faulty unit.

His maintenance request reached Roy, who was already in the building.

'Marching orders at seven o'clock. It's like being back in the army.'

'I didn't sleep either,' said Roy, as he fixed the light once more. It's why I came in early.'

'So, you're not on duty? ... officially?'

'Not for an hour.'

Devereux pointed at the visitor chair. Roy sat with a sigh. 'Were you in the army, then?'

'It's a figure of speech. May I ask how old you are?'

'Twenty-one.'

'Which month?'

'End of June, or beginning of July.'

'What an intriguing answer.'

Roy related the story of his 'birth' - dumped outside the Police Station in a bag for life.

'Extraordinary, a genuine foundling.'

Roy talked about his early life, comfortably confiding in a man who'd soon be taking all these confidences to the grave. He said what he could remember about his early adoptive parents and his time in the children's home. He was more reluctant to say anything about his year in the young offender institution; he'd rather leave those memories buried. Devereux continued to question the young man, aware that his one-hour conversation was almost through. Roy finally told his story.

'I knew a couple of them, but the driver was new to me. The offer was a cavort out of town. I had nothing else to do. So, anyway, the driver was a bit of a nut. I wanted to get out of the car, but the others took the mickey. We stopped at a farm shop. I didn't want anything - and anyway, I didn't have any money. They went in, came out and whoosh, we hit the road. I realised straightaway that something was wrong. No-one made a sound. One went down for GBH and the rest of us were sentenced for 'joint enterprise'. I expect you know what that is.'

'I do,' replied Devereux quietly. 'It was a lousy law.'

'I didn't hurt anyone,' insisted Roy.

'I believe you.'

'I got eighteen months. Out in nine. I came back to town. I lived in a beach hut for a while. Food was easy ... that was when supermarkets were still dumping stuff in their bins.' Roy was silent for over a minute. He smiled and sat up. 'Then, amazing really, a job and somewhere to live. Someone was watching over me.' Devereux leaned forward and spoke more purposefully.

'Roy, there's something I'd like you to do for me.'

After hurrying through his morning chores and grabbing a bite to eat, Roy left especially early for his morning patient run. His first address was Lapwing Cottage, Devereux's home on the creek. Roy felt slightly uncomfortable as he took Devereux's keyring from his pocket and entered the empty property. With the window shutters closed, it took a few moments to see the sparsely-furnished room. A figure standing in the darkness was merely a pair of binoculars on a tall tripod. A pile of charred papers had been blown from the fireplace, pockmarking the tiled floor. Roy instinctively reached for a broom and swept the ashes in to a neat pile. Fragments of photographs had survived the fire: a smiling face, an outstretched arm and a child running from camera. He located the antique chest of drawers described by Devereux and removed the requested leather briefcase. He pushed lightly against a door, curious to see the rest of the cottage. He was checked by his conscience. He'd done what was asked of him. Roy locked the front door and glanced around to see if he was being watched. With his patients safely delivered to the hospice day centre, Roy climbed the stairs to Side Room Six. He presented Devereux with the briefcase. The man ran his hands affectionately across the leather.

'Thank you. This is where I kept all my precious things.'

'I didn't open it. I didn't look inside.'

'Of course not. What else did you see while you were there?'

'A couple of geese ... and an egret when I was driving back.'

'Which type?'

'Great white.'

'Lucky you. One can see so many birds on the creek. Lapwing Cottage is the perfect hide. Thanks again.'

Roy turned in the doorway and handed the keyring back to Devereux. When he was alone, the man opened the leather case and looked inside; the case was empty.

CHAPTER THIRTEEN

A police car in the hospice carpark was never a good sign. Roy steered clear of the vehicle and rode his bike through the automatic doors. The new receptionist called after him.

'Excuse me, are you Roy Birch? You're to go to Mrs King's office ... immediately.'

Another bad sign. Roy secured his bike in the store room and ran up the stairs. The manager sat at her desk. The crumpled Detective stood to one side.

'Hello Roy, good to see you again.'

Mrs King quickly interrupted, to explain her presence. 'Roy, dear. The police wish to speak with you informally. I'm here to represent your interests. Do you know what an appropriate adult is?'

'I've known a few,' Roy replied joylessly.

'This is a voluntary interview,' she continued. 'It's a matter of safeguarding. You'll remember we've talked about that.'

'Yes. Sure. OK.'

'Why do you think I'm here, Roy?' asked the Detective quietly.

'I don't think you know, do you?' suggested Mrs King. The Detective raised a silencing hand and smiled at Roy.

'I'm sure you have some idea.'

'Not my bike.'

'No, not your bike.'

The Detective took a photograph from a thick document file and placed it on the desk. It was a police custody shot of the elfin woman, complete with height markings behind her head.

'Do you recognise this person?'

'Yes. Has she been arrested?'

'This was taken last year. When did you last see this woman?'

'A couple of weeks ago.'

'Where was this?'

As the questions continued, Roy brought into mind one of the coin arcade attractions that had fascinated him so much as a child. A coin dropped into the funnel would spin around the spiral, getting faster and faster, before disappearing down the central hole. This is what he felt like now, seemingly incriminating himself with every answer. The elfin woman had been murdered: hit repeatedly with a blunt instrument. A second body had been discovered in the same location.

'Beano?' stammered Roy. The Detective took a second photograph from his file – a custody photograph of Beano, standing before the same height chart. 'This must be old too,' insisted Roy. 'He's got a scar on his face now. Has he been killed as well?'

Mrs King closed her eyes momentarily, unhappy with Roy's candour. The Detective closed his file. The interview would continue on the following day – at the police station. He placed Roy's phone inside an evidence bag. Roy was glad to be rid of it.

Roy wanted to hide under his bed or crawl under a stone. He did the next best thing. Cleaning the mortuary floor gave him time to think. He felt at home in the land of the dead. The second murder was not Beano, but Napoleon, his morose companion. This was surely Beano's doing. The three of them were in it together ... whatever 'it' was. He would learn more tomorrow, not that he wanted to learn anything more. Was he next in the firing line? Without his phone,

Roy had to return to the facilities office every twenty minutes and wait for further instructions. Bernice served the usual stack of starch for lunch, but he'd lost his appetite. With a full refrigerator, he was kept busy assisting various funeral directors. Their casual exchanges all went unheard. Going home time was a welcome relief. He did take a couple of wrong turnings, but none of his passengers complained; they were in no hurry to get anywhere. Returning to the hospice carpark, Roy spotted a figure staring at him from the window of Side Room Six. This was no elfin woman, or the ghost of a woman. It appeared to be a tall, bald man, dressed in black. Roy sat still in the driving seat, waiting for a cloud to pass and clear his vision. The tall man was still staring directly at him from the window. It felt like a premonition. It was not a good sign.

Roy completed his afternoon tasks and walked up to the ward with some trepidation. When he was a kid, he was told that an angel appears when someone dies. Perhaps Devereux had been taken. He was relieved to see light spilling from Side Room Six. Devereux was engrossed in his book. Roy was off the clock. He slouched on the visitor chair.

'Hungry?' asked Devereux.

'Very.'

'I had a visitor this afternoon and he left me a selection of delicious things. Unfortunately, my gut's not up to it.'

Roy accepted the small wicker hamper and looked in wonder at the fine items: cheese, biscuits, nuts, preserves and chocolate truffles.

'Are you sure?'

'Knock yourself out.'

Roy broke in to a pack of roasted pecans. 'Your visitor ... is he a tall man? ... no hair?'

'That's the man. I was hoping to introduce you to him, but you weren't answering your phone.'

'The police took it.'

Devereux already knew about the murders. It had been reported on the national news.

'You can tell me as much as you want, Roy ... but, if I could give you a bit of advice, tell the police *everything* you know. No partial answers. As soon as they think you're hiding something, they'll get their teeth into you. Do you understand?'

'I know they do that,' replied Roy, as he bit into a truffle.

Mrs King drove Roy to the police station. Roy had never seen her outside the hospice. She looked smaller than usual, driving hesitantly through the morning traffic.

'Remember what I said ... no comment or can't remember. Let's avoid the need for a solicitor.'

The police interview room was crowded. Roy and Mrs King faced the crumpled Detective and two other officers. A smartly-dressed Detective Inspector from South London resembled a bird of prey, with light blue eyes and sleek, raven-black hair. Her Detective Sergeant was also nattily dressed in a tailored suit. Roy held nothing back during the recorded interview. Used to the routine, he anticipated many of the officers' questions, carefully describing his encounters with Napoleon, Beano and the elfin woman. Dates, times and witnesses at the Seashell Café were noted. He described getting lost on Church Street and Church Row on the night of the murders. The CCTV footage of Roy corroborated.

'Have you ever acted as a courier?'

'I don't know. For what?'

'Has anyone ever asked you to take a package to a particular address, or collect one?'

Roy hesitated. The Detective Inspector leaned forward. 'Yes, but not like you're thinking.' Roy told them about Devereux briefcase in precise detail.

'Is that it? The only occasion? Have you visited London or Brighton?'

'Never,' he replied truthfully. 'I'm guessing this is about drugs.'

'I wouldn't want you to guess anything, Roy. I'm going to say a few words. I want you to tell me if they mean anything to you. Cannabinoid'

'Nothing.'

'Precursor.'

'Nothing.'

'Nitazene.'

'Nita, what? No, Nothing.'

The Detective Inspector narrowed her eyes, then placed seven photographs in a row.

'Tell me which of these individuals you recognise.' Roy pointed at a familiar face. 'This is the boy who was found in Half Moon Alley.'

'Do you know what a trap house is?'

'No, I don't.'

When the hour-long interview drew to a close, the crumpled Detective took Roy's phone from an evidence bag and handed it back.

'You'll be needing this.'

Mrs King was furious. Her knuckles were almost white on the steering wheel. Roy didn't know if she was more concerned about his fate, or losing an invaluable member of staff.

'Going behind my back. Running errands for patients. What were you thinking? This will draw a lot of unwelcome attention. You should have brought this to *me*,' She added in a more conciliatory tone. 'We could have managed this.'

Mrs King reversed in to her reserved space and killed the engine. She looked fondly at the hospice building.

'You do like it here, don't you?'

'It's practically my home,' replied Roy. 'I don't know where else I could be.'

'There's a career here. You have fine prospects. Don't throw it all away.'

Agnieszka was happy to be gifted some luxuries from Devereux's food hamper. She too had some advice.

'Don't get too friendly with the patients. You get close and then they're gone. Be nice, but not ... you know what I mean. That actress and now this man Devereux. You'll get depressed.'

Roy was already depressed. He'd heard the word 'don't' enough times for one day. As he refuelled the minibus, he noticed the billboard had at last been changed. It now announced, COUNTY LINES DOUBLE MURDER. There would soon be details. The reports would feature stark crime scene pictures and reveal details of the killings. Roy felt sick at the thought. When his phone rang, his heart skipped a beat – it was only Devereux.

Devereux raised his stick and closed the door of Side Room Six. He turned to Roy, who was hunched on the visitor chair.

'I know who they should be looking for,' insisted Roy.

'Slow down. Take a deep breath. Show me your phone.' Devereux opened the clamshell device and examined it closely. 'Are you certain that this is the phone you gave to them yesterday?'

'I'm positive, I know every scratch.'

The two men sat in silence for minutes.

'Talk to me, Roy.'

And did he talk. As if he was inside a confessional, Roy's inhibitions fell away. The constant need to be on guard, to second guess the motives of everyone he encountered, was forgotten.

'It doesn't sound as if you're a suspect, Devereux said reassuringly. The police have your DNA. If they had any evidence from the crime scene, you'd be in custody. They're hoping that you will lead them to this Beano character. The police will monitor every call on your phone. Come and tell me about anything unusual, but, and this is very important, *never* call my number.'

It was almost dark when Roy pushed his bike out of the hospice entrance. He'd missed his literacy evening class, but he didn't care. How inconsequential that seemed to him now. He spent the evening poring over his well-thumbed bird books, determined to distract himself. The swallows migrated to Africa at the end of the summer. He wished he too could spread his wings and escape. During the police interview, the Detective Inspector had told him not to leave the country. He'd smiled at the idea. He knew you needed a passport to do that. He reached to his hamper and speared the last fig in syrup. As if drugged by its sweetness, he fell in to an unnaturally deep sleep.

Agnieszka bought both of the local newspapers to glean what she could on the double murder. Lurid details of bludgeoning and suffocation made her wince, but she was determined to read every word. And there it was at last; the police photograph of Benedict Knowles (aka Beano aka Benny aka Beaky). This person of interest was, 'Not to be approached,' barked Agnieszka. 'He may be armed.' Roy remained silent, as he finished repairing a patient bedside table. His phone was heavy in his pocket all day, but it didn't receive a single call. When he left the hospice for home, he felt ten times lighter.

With a single, small bouquet to deliver, Roy's Saturday trip to the cemetery barely covered the cost of fuel. 'Your pain is over,' read the card.

'He's at two o'clock,' said a passing undertaker. 'There's been a real mix up on the timings. A double booking. And this lot are already five minutes over.' The song 'My Way' reached a distorted crescendo on the sound system. The undertaker snuffed out his cigarette. 'Here we go. Showtime.'

Roy wandered up to the row of recent burials. He was pleased to see that Frances now had a shining headstone. He opened his phone to take a photograph, then realised it was probably unwise, given the circumstances. Back at his bedsit, he unpacked his laundered sheets and clothes. There were no hidden gifts this week. The Marias had spotted the visiting police car and had heard about the murders in their town - Roy was to be held at arm's for the time being. Even Gina didn't look him straight in the eye. And what if it is me next, he thought. Will anyone come to my funeral? ... or will they stay away, because it's probably what I deserved. It was no use hiding out at home. He walked to the seafront, to flush his rankling thoughts. On Sunday afternoon, he watched half a movie at The Picturedrome. He wondered why the characters called themselves heroes, when all they seemed to do was kill people. It was too late to do anything else and too early to call it a night. Roy collected his bike and rode to the hospice.

Devereux was pleased and surprised to see Roy giving up his precious time for a Sunday evening visit. The BBC evening service echoed through the ward. Precious Adaugo turned up the volume when her favourite hymn was selected.

'See what I mean? At least she never plays a requiem, said Devereux with a resigned smile.'

'It's the first time I've been in on a Sunday. It feels different somehow.'

'Does it. All days feel the same to me.'

'How *are* you feeling?'

'Kind of you to ask. Not good. The cancer cells are doing what they're good at.' Devereux held up his fists in a Queensbury Rules boxing pose. 'Every third thought shall be my grave.'

'I was passing,' Roy explained.

'Join the club.'

Roy felt awkward. Perhaps he shouldn't have come; it was a bad idea. Their conversation had been so easy and natural before, but there was now an uneasy silence.

'Perhaps I should ...'

'No, please don't go,' Devereux interjected. Devereux twisted in his chair and closed his eyes. Roy was about to leave the room when Devereux started speaking. 'I had a son. His name was Jack. He was the same age as you, to the month.' Roy waited for more, but the man was silent.

'Have you got a picture of him?' asked Roy.

'I don't as it happens. I looked at the photographs too often. It became wearisome.'

'What happened to him?'

'It was just before his eighth birthday. His mother and I were planning a party for his friends. He was a popular boy. That summer, he was always wearing a pair of those jelly sandals. I'm sure you've seen the kind of thing. They were made of a very soft plastic. See-through green. He never bothered to secure the strap, he just dragged his feet - 'You're going to trip if you're not careful, Jack'. Anyway, he climbed onto the roof of an old orangery, attached to the side of the house. It still had all of its Victorian glass. I told Jack I was going to restore it soon. It was going to be a den for him and his pals. Yes, he climbed onto the old roof supports, and, for some inexplicable reason, decided to walk the length of the ridge, from one side to the other. And he was wearing those jelly shoes.' After a long silence, Devereux spoke again. 'Those stupid shoes.'

CHAPTER FOURTEEN

On Monday there was a short-lived drama; electrical power had been lost to the entire building. Mrs King tried switch after switch before she allowed herself to believe. She was short with Agnieszka, expecting the facilities manager to restore power at will. Her primary concern was the mortuary refrigerator. Funeral Directors were told to collect their respective bodies as soon as possible. One was unlikely to be collected for days, as the deceased was due to be repatriated to The Caribbean. The flight had been booked, but the paperwork was not yet finalised.

'It's not our concern,' muttered Mrs King repeatedly. 'They should keep their clients on their premises. What's the temperature now?'

Roy was given the task of checking. Since the fridge temperature panel was known to be unreliable, he was required to shine a torch at the domestic thermometer hanging from a piece of string between two of the bodies.

'And don't leave the doors open.' Insisted Agnieszka from the outside corridor. 'We'll lose even more heat ... I mean cold.'

The refrigerator belched loudly and the room filled with light. It made Roy jump. Had Agnieszka been in the room, she would probably have fainted.

'The corridor lights have just come back on,' announced Agnieszka. Do you have power in there?'

'Back to life,' answered Roy.

Mrs King thanked Agnieszka and Roy effusively, as if they had done something to fix the problem. There was a brief chat about purchasing a generator, but Mrs King's eyes glazed over when she heard the estimated cost. Roy was more concerned about the Genesis III – would the ancient boiler be able to wake itself up? He discovered the controls were working normally and hot water was flowing. He thought of his disappointed friend Norton and hoped he was at peace, whatever that meant. At lunchtime, Roy picked the gristle out of his meat and thought how strange it was for the dead to be flown around the world to be buried. How many air passengers eating and enjoying themselves knew a dead body was stowed next to their suitcases, just below their seats? His phone vibrated: light out in Side Room Six.

The first thing that struck Roy was Devereux's thin voice. It no longer emanated from his chest, but from somewhere near his throat. He pulled the visitor chair closer, in order to hear.

'Any more anonymous calls? To your phone?'

'Not yet.'

'I've been thinking a good deal about your life, Roy. Here's an important question for you ... how do we know whom to trust?'

'You mean with secrets?'

'In general.'

'I don't know. I've never been good at it.'

'And that's got you in to trouble.'

'I suppose that's the reason, yes.'

'Come back after work, or Mrs King will give me one of her withering looks. She thinks I'm a bed blocker. Come back at the end of your day.'

Roy returned to Side Room Six at five o'clock. Devereux rattled on for an hour, repeating fragments of anecdotes and commenting on people and places

Roy had never heard of. He occasionally asked Roy a pertinent question about his life and nodded sagely.

'You'd better go now, Roy. Stay away from me until I send for you and remember, *never* call my number.'

There were moments during the week when Roy wished he could push the side room door open a few inches and check on Devereux, but he kept away as requested. Whenever he parked the minibus, Roy looked up to the window of Side Room Six. He had two brief sightings of the tall, bald man in black. Friend or angel, the visitor clearly had some right to be in the room.

Roy thought he may never see the patient again, so it was a surprise when, three days later, Devereux played the lightbulb trick one more time. He spoke quietly and urgently, requesting Roy to return to the side room that evening at five, on the dot. He was to stay as long as instructed.

'Do you understand, Roy? Repeat what I've just said.'

Roy wasn't particularly fazed by Devereux's mysterious instructions. He'd heard many anxious patients issue strange commands. Perhaps Devereux didn't want to be alone. He returned at the specified time and sat uneasily on the visitor seat. Devereux asked Roy to open the door, in order to be seen by passing staff.

'Who's on duty tonight?'

'It's Precious, with a couple of agency nurses. They're regulars.'

'Good. Good. Please change the water in my jug. Make sure Precious sees what you're doing. Make a point of asking her the time. Trust me.'

Roy complied to this and other requests to make himself conspicuous during the evening.

'Do you believe in heaven?' Asked Roy.

'Heaven and hell. It's merely fear and superstition. The world and everything in it is governed by the laws of nature, not gods.'

'Then what's the point of trying to be good?'

'Roy, that's probably the greatest philosophical question ... and there's no simple answer. When you were at Lapwing Cottage, did you notice a green vase on the mantel? Never mind, you may look at it again one day. The day my son Jack died, I knocked it to the floor. Not intentionally. I was probably careering around the room. An old pal of mine specialised in invisible repair. Let me tell you, there's no such thing. One needs to be reminded of the break, not have it conveniently erased. The Japanese understand this. They practice something called Kintsugi, which means golden joinery. When you look at the vase, notice the lines of gold dust and lacquer. That's where my son now lives - not in any heaven.'

They continued to converse occasionally, but Devereux was growing weaker by the hour. At two o'clock the following morning, Devereux's phone rang quietly.

'Yes?' Devereux listened for one minute, then answered his caller. 'I understand. Good night, old friend.' Devereux switched off his phone and leaned back heavily. His shoulders lowered into the chair. 'Every third thought becomes every other thought becomes the only thought. I'm loath to leave, but there it is.'

'Should I go now?' asked Roy.

Devereux managed a confirming wave and switched out his reading light. Roy didn't like the idea of cycling home. He had no lights and he'd only wake Gina, his landlady. He lay on a punctured air mattress in the facilities office. He stayed awake, trying to make sense of the unusual day. He was just managing to drop off, when a scratching sound drew his attention. By the light under the door, he could see it was Confirmatory Medical Certificate: Charles Andre Devereux, 69 years, stage 4 metastatic adenocarcinoma of the colon (liver metastasis), 03:10, exhaustion.

Roy stood still at the centre of the room for twenty minutes, then sat at his desk and carefully cleaned a mortice lock.

The news broke at one o'clock that afternoon. A person of interest in the county lines murder enquiry had been found dead. Agnieszka twisted her monitor, so Roy could see the national television broadcast. The reporter was explaining that Benedict Knowles had been discovered at first light, slumped next to a promenade shelter. The police had been hoping to locate Knowles; they believed his death could be related to three previous murders in the town. The reporter was still talking when Roy was told to go to Mrs King's office immediately.

'You are not under arrest,' said the London Detective Inspector, who'd hotfooted it down to the coast. Her remark did not reassure Roy, who was the only one seated in the room; it certainly felt like a formal interview. 'Four deaths within one square mile. You must have your own ideas.'

'Your own suspicions? ... of other people,' suggested Mrs King.

'I'm sure you know that it's a crime to withhold information,' added the Detective. 'Tell me where you were between eight-fifteen and eleven-fifteen last night.'

Roy told the Detective about his long evening visit to Side Room Six.

'We'll speak with Mr Devereux to confirm. You do understand that.'

'Mr Devereux passed away,' said Mrs King. 'Three o'clock this morning ... or thereabouts.'

'Not a very good alibi then,' replied the Detective.

Roy explained that Precious Adaugo had come into the room twice during the evening, concerned for Mr Devereux's privacy. Roy had also spoken to the two other nurses on the ward.

'How did Beano die?' asked Roy.

'Roy ...,' interjected Mrs King, as if her employee was some kind of embarrassment. 'Just answer the Inspector's questions.'

'How did he die?' Roy repeated, ignoring his manager's rebuke.

'You'll know when we know. Meanwhile, you know the drill. Stay in the town. Do you have any questions?'

'Yes. Can my next interview be at the police station ... recorded ... and with a solicitor?'

Mrs King looked deflated.

Roy's main task of the day was to decommission Side Room Six. The furniture was removed and all electrical items disabled. Agnieszka was determined that the haunted room should only be used as a last resort. Roy was told to take the patient's wing chair to the charity shop, where it was quickly appropriated by a volunteer. He laid claim to Devereux's books; they would have pride of place in his collection.

Going home time was unsettling for Roy. All of the passengers discussed their theories about the recent death: the words 'murder' and 'gangs' were bandied about. Returning to the hospice carpark, he discovered another police car. Passing the refectory, he observed a uniformed officer and Bernice having an earnest conversation. Agnieszka declined to say what she said in her own statement. Roy felt the sand was shifting beneath his feet. Finally, the night staff arrived for their shift; all three nurses verified his story: his alibi was bulletproof.

Saturday morning brought new discomfort. There was no wakeup call from Gina. She loaded her wreathes into the delivery van and left quietly for the cemetery. Roy did find some consolation at the Seashell Café, where the owner still gave him free coffees and snacks. He rode along the promenade to the shelter where Beano's body was discovered. There were no flowers or tea lights here, just the remaining metre of blue and white police tape fluttering in the breeze. He wandered along the deserted seafront and through the emptying streets until dusk.

'Tell me, O muse, of that ingenious hero who travelled far and wide after he had sacked the famous town of Troy. Many cities did he visit, and many were the nations with whose ...'

Roy returned his new, old book to the shelf and flicked through a copy of Reader's Digest, in search of some missed wisdom. His discovery seemed providential, *'No person was ever honoured for what he received. Honour has been the reward for what he gave'*. He carefully cut out the text and placed it inside his shoebox of quotes.

The main event on Monday morning was the collection of Devereux's body. Roy went to the mortuary early, to spend some time alone with the old man. For the first time, Roy noticed three livid scars on the abdomen and chest – uneven stitching traced old injuries. In his shroud, Devereux resembled a hero slain in battle. He lay in state for minutes, before Roy's phone announced the private ambulance's arrival.

'Hello, Roy,' grinned Holly. 'You've let your hair grow back ... looks nice.' The two women from City Funeral Directors steered their trolley into the mortuary.

'Oh, I remember him,' commented Holly's colleague. 'He was quite a character. He came in to make all his own arrangements.'

'Treat him with honour.' Roy said solemnly. He couldn't understand why he would say such a thing and felt slightly embarrassed. The two women exchanged a kind look and transferred the body. The older woman gave him a banknote.

'When's the funeral? I want to be there.' Asked Roy.

'It's a direct cremation. No-one allowed to attend. He was very emphatic.'

As she wheeled the trolley away, Holly turned and smiled again.

'See you, Roy.'

Roy pushed the money deep into his pocket. This was not common currency to be squandered on Agnieszka's treats; it was Devereux's gift to the ferryman.

Roy opened the book of remembrance to a fresh page. He wrote a tribute to Devereux in his neatest handwriting, 'He taught me not to fear death. Heaven is fear and superstition'. The rest of the week was mercifully uneventful, just half-remembered faces and predictable days. Another memorial bench arrived, to be stored in the basement with all of its protective bubble wrap in place, 'Our loving mother – always remembered'. Roy remembered to switch the lights out as he locked the basement door. He wanted to add 'always remembered' to his Devereux tribute. He was disappointed to find the relevant page had been torn out of the book of condolences. Later that day, a familiar hand gripped his arm. The Chaplain spoke with deliberate calmness and assumed authority.

'It's a difficult time, Roy. When you need a shoulder, or just an ear ... I'm here.'

'I wish you'd leave me alone.'

'That is a very understandable response,' The Chaplain replied unabashed. 'Grief is a mysterious process.'

The circulation of local newspapers rose again. Both publications featured two-page spreads filled with speculation about Benedict Knowles' death.

'DRUGS WAR TEARS TOWN TO PIECES,' announced Agnieszka in her upper case voice. 'The investigation is proceeding at pace. Local police are working closely with the Metropolitan Police. You don't get a mention,' she added with relief. Roy left the facilities room and sought privacy on the roof. He sat on the permanently stuck chair and considered the facts: forensic examination of Beano's DNA placed him in the trap house. Isn't it likely that he was the killer? If that was the case, then who killed him? Or did anyone kill him? Despite having small quantities of amphetamines in his blood, they were not the cause of death – and the post mortem was inconclusive. When Roy returned to the office, he found a letter addressed to him, placed very neatly on his swivel chair. Agnieszka looked over the top of her newspaper.

'Nice writing. What does it say?'

Roy folded the unopened letter and put it in his back pocket, where it remained until going home time. With the last patient delivered he read and reread the very brief handwritten note.

Roy was clearly back in The Marias' good books. When he collected his laundry, they presented him with a mug: his name in gold script and the astrological birth sign of Pisces. They were a few months out, but he appreciated the gesture. A portrait of Roy holding his mug was forwarded to the niece in Manila.

CHAPTER FIFTEEN

A friendly voice woke Roy at eight.

'Three services, my love. First is at nine-forty,' trumpeted Gina.

Roy washed and dressed hurriedly, revitalised by his apparent reinstatement. He laid out the Saturday wreathes and bouquets behind the crematorium, then returned directly to his bedsit. Wearing his suit, he joined a group of passengers at the bus stop, where all eyes were fixed expectantly on the horizon. Someone helped him decipher the bus timetable, before adding gloomily, 'Not that this means anything. They just come when they want.' Roy looked repeatedly at his phone during the journey, concerned that he would be late for his meeting. As he gazed at the passing countryside, his spirits rose. He'd occasionally seen the tip of the cathedral spire on his daily runs, but today it ascended majestically to its full height, welcoming him to the city. With one hour to kill, he circled the ancient building in wonder. 'Some people believe in heaven,' he whispered.

Using the letter's hand drawn map, he navigated the narrow side streets and found the ancient building. He ran his finger across a brass plaque: Cairncross & Lowe – Family Solicitors. Ringing the bell brought an immediate response. Roy was taken aback when the tall, bald man in black appeared in the doorway. Roy held up the letter, as if it was an entry ticket.

'Mr Cairncross ...'

'Roy Birch' boomed the solicitor. 'Andrew. Always Andrew to my favoured clients.' The man turned and marched briskly up the narrow wooden staircase. 'Mind your head. People were a lot shorter in the sixteenth century.' Andrew ducked as he entered his wood-panelled office, where two large desks faced each other. 'Take the weight off your feet.' Roy sank into a magnificent Chesterfield chair.

'Why are you here?'

'You sent me a note ...'

'Rhetorical, Roy. I thought it better to meet away from your workplace. We can both be more candid.'

'Who knew I needed a solicitor?'

'Charles. Charles Devereux.'

'Brilliant. Will it be free? Pro bono?'

'I can see you're not new to this. It's Harriet who does our crime. You're sitting in her chair. No, don't get up.'

'So, you don't do crime?'

'Not if I can help it,' answered Andrew, stony-faced. I'm a family solicitor – divorce, adoptions, trusts, child custody. That sort of thing. And of course, estates. You made quite an impression on Charles. He was struck by your disposition.'

Andrew described his final conversations with his old friend, whom he met in the armed forces.

'Were you in the army?'

'The Parachute Regiment. Anyway, it seems Charles wants to take you under his wing. Before we begin ... when did you last eat?' Roy's hesitation said it all. Andrew bowled him along another narrow corridor into a neighbouring building. 'Head head! I don't want you to sue me if you get knocked out.' The adjoining Elizabethan room was barely able to accommodate the dining room table and chairs. The various trays of cheeses, fruits and salads looked inviting.

'Dig in. Talk as we eat. Charles told me you like birds. He was mad about them. I remember we were once in a foxhole half way up a mountain. Look! Twenty metres at ten-o'clock, he said, it's a scrub sparrow. He put out crumbs for this bird and a whole flock turned up. Damn near gave our position away.'

'What do you want from me?' Roy asked, almost apologetically. Andrew stopped reminiscing and poured two coffees.

'Some quickfire questions. Do you have a contract of employment?'

'As you requested.' Roy tapped his pocket.

'A tenancy agreement? ... for your flat? A bank account? Do you know your HMRC tax code? Dental practice?' Roy shook his head after every question. 'Are you registered with a GP Surgery?'

'I should think so.'

'We suspected as much. Who organises all your affairs?'

'Mrs King does everything.'

'It certainly seems that way.'

Andrew tactfully explained that Charles wanted to help him become more self-sufficient. If Roy were to give his permission, Andrew would be pleased to act as his solicitor.

'It would merely be a standard enquiry at this stage, to ensure that everything is in your best interest.' The solicitor explained every paragraph of a short form consent. Without hesitation, Roy settled the pen in his left hand and signed the document.

'Why is there no funeral for Mr Devereux? I wanted to go.'

'It's a sensitive business. Some of the chaps who might attend are still in service. And we know that others who attend are there to identify them. It's a security issue. I'm sure you'll understand.'

Travelling back to his home town, Roy watched the cathedral spire sink in to the landscape, followed by the setting sun. What had he just set in motion? Had he grassed on Mrs King? The last thing he wanted was to get her in to any trouble; she'd given him everything. Mr Cairncross had reimbursed his bus fare, which was a good start. He felt he should trust the man.

Roy needn't have worried. Mrs King couldn't have been nicer. Her dry office meetings were replaced with friendly sessions in the garden. She brought him up to date with her submissions to his solicitor and was uncharacteristically generous when Roy wanted a day off to return to the city.

'Take two days. You deserve it. You've been under a lot of pressure lately.'

Roy returned to the city two weeks later. He weaved his way through the bustling market crowd and found the discreet doorway. He was warned that the meeting with Andrew and his legal partner would take a few hours, including their working lunch.

'I'm taking minutes, so you won't need to take notes ... but just in case.' Harriet Lowe handed Roy a handsomely-bound notebook. He ran his figure over the embossed company name, Cairncross & Lowe. She settled into her Chesterfield and prepared to write. Andrew turned various pages, to refresh his memory.

'To the matter, Roy. When you were fifteen years of age you left your second set of adoptive parents. You then - please stop me at any time if anything I say is incorrect - you returned to the care of children's social services. When you were eighteen, Social Services put a transition plan in place for your move in to adult life.

'They gave me some leaflet. Benefits. How to find employment. It didn't really work out.'

'When you were nineteen, you were convicted and spent nine months at a young offender institution.'

Roy felt as if he was back in court. He stared at the intricately-designed Turkish carpet.

'And you've never had contact with either of your parents?'

'Never.'

'To all intents and purposes, Mrs King has acted as your guardian for the last nine months. Here's the rub, Roy. Although your employer is abiding by the terms of your contract, they are dealing with your interests in an unconventional way. Your monthly salary is staying in the hospice accounts. The manager pays you ... and your landlady from petty cash. She's also deducting payments for all of your meals. In short, you have no savings. If I was less charitable, I'd think of it as indentured servitude.'

'I knew it. I've got her in to trouble, haven't I?'

‘Not necessarily.’ Andrew’s voice became warmer. ‘She put a roof over your head. And look at the service she offers the community. I think we should cut her some slack, don’t you? She’s prepared a new contract with retrospective compensation. We’ll go through that later.’

‘Will I lose my bedsit?’

‘We’ll come to that. You did bring your driving licence?’

Roy patted his jacket pocket. ‘Good. Harriet’s going to take you to the bank across the street and help you open two bank accounts – current and savings; they’ll be registered at this address. During lunch in the adjoining dining room, Roy was made to feel at home. This is just like a real family, thought Roy. In both of his placements, the people who adopted him never ate meals together. Harriet talked about her children and said that Roy would meet them one day. He began to feel slightly uncomfortable. There was so much talk about the future. He didn’t fully understand what was going on. Why were these solicitors giving him so much of their time? The trio returned to the office with their coffee and continued the day’s business.

'Roy, I'm planning to retire next year,' confided Andrew. 'Keep it under your hat. When I do, Harriet will be looking after your affairs – your de facto guardian.'

'Next year?' Roy took some comfort from the thought, but did not know what to say next.

'And the coming years,' added Andrew. 'Charles Devereux set-up a trust, that will become active when you're twenty-two years of age. It's not a huge sum, but it will afford you more opportunities. There is a condition ... that you continue with further education, either full term or in an apprenticeship. What's your feeling about that?'

'What would I learn?'

'The choice is yours.'

'I want to work in funerals.'

'Perfect. Exactly what Charles thought. You asked me about your bedsit. Harriet will take care of your rent. However, there's another matter ...' Andrew tore open an envelope and let a keyring drop into his hand. 'I believe you have visited Lapwing Cottage.'

'Yes, Mr Devereux's home.'

'Well, it's your home now ... if you want it. It's not yours to sell, but you have a life tenancy. That's a hell of a gift, if I might say so. Charles has no family. He was an extraordinarily generous man.'

Andrew handed the keyring to Roy, who held the keys tightly in his clenched fist. He looked shaken.

'Are you all right?' asked Harriet. Roy nodded and caught his breath. The three sat in silence for a minute.

'And there is one more matter,' Andrew said with a note of uncertainty. 'Something that does not require an answer now. It requires a lot of thought. It was a hope, not a request. Charles would like it if you changed your name to Devereux ... if *you* would like to.'

'Roy Devereux,' whispered Roy.

The following day, Roy cycled to the creek. A skein of noisy Canada geese pointed him in the right direction. His heart skipped a beat as he entered Lapwing Cottage. The door, that he dare not open on his last visit, led into a kitchen. He caught sight of his reflection in a tall, steel refrigerator. Another key opened the back door. Roy stepped out to a garden, where blooms and grasses bowed towards him. At the far end stood an apple tree, surrounded by windfalls.

A metal sign of remembrance was firmly planted next to the trunk. Roy cleaned the plaque and read the inscription aloud.

Jack Samuel Devereux
Our little life is rounded with a sleep

Roy picked up one of the apples, wiped it on his sleeve and took a bite. It was the sweetest fruit he'd ever eaten.

***

Printed in Great Britain
by Amazon

63237443R10114